# SEE: LOSS.
# SEE ALSO: LOVE.

A Novel

# Yukiko Tominaga

SCRIBNER

NEW YORK   LONDON   TORONTO   SYDNEY   NEW DELHI

Scribner
An Imprint of Simon & Schuster, LLC
1230 Avenue of the Americas
New York, NY 10020

First Scribner hardcover edition May 2024

SCRIBNER and design are trademarks of Simon & Schuster, LLC

Simon & Schuster: Celebrating 100 Years of Publishing in 2024

For information about special discounts for bulk purchases,
please contact Simon & Schuster Special Sales at
1-866-506-1949 or business@simonandschuster.com.

The Simon & Schuster Speakers Bureau can bring authors to your live event. For more information or to book an event, contact the Simon & Schuster Speakers Bureau at 1-866-248-3049 or visit our website at www.simonspeakers.com.

Interior design by Kathryn A. Kenney-Peterson

Manufactured in the United States of America

10   9   8   7   6   5   4   3   2   1

Library of Congress Cataloging-in-Publication Data is available.

ISBN 978-1-6680-3167-4
ISBN 978-1-6680-3169-8 (ebook)

The following chapters of this book were previously published as short stories: "My Father," *Bellingham Review*, 2019; "Missing: adjective; absent—see: lost," *Chicago Quarterly Review*, 2017; "My Jewish Genie," originally published as "The First-Year Mourner," *North Dakota Quarterly*, 2017; "The Death of the Fish," *Oxford Magazine*, 2016; "Nukegara," *Passages North*, 2013

*For my bubbe*

# TABLE OF CONTENTS

## 破裂 (*haretsu*): rupture

## 渦 (*uzu*): vortex

## 界面 (*kaimen*): interface

# 創発 (*souhatsu*): **emergence**

# SEE: LOSS.
# SEE ALSO: LOVE.

# 破裂 (*haretsu*):
# rupture

# Missing: adjective; absent—see: lost

IN JAPANESE, WE HAD NO ACTUAL TRANSLATION FOR "I MISS YOU." THE direct translation had become extinct, no longer a part of our conversations, existing only in romance novels. The sentence that we substituted was "I'll be lonely without you." But when we said it, we reflexively abandoned "I" and "without you," leaving "Will be lonely." Which of us became lonely because of the other's absence wasn't explicit. We left it to the air to take care of the rest, as if releasing the words was enough to understand one another. These three words floated like bubbles between two people, sharing the moment until the bubbles burst and blended into the world.

"I'll be lonely without you" was a mistranslation because missing someone didn't necessarily mean you would be lonely. Missing someone came from the outside. A momentary fact. It was innocent and healthy. Once you moved from the moment, you stopped missing, while loneliness stayed within you like a virus. It mutated, and only distractions allowed us to survive.

When I explained this to my mother-in-law, Bubbe, she shook her head and said, "Japanese people—so specific yet so vague."

"At least we make reliable cars," I said.

"Cars have nothing to do with human emotion."

I laughed and told her our conversation should go into the story that I was writing for my class.

"Do you ever miss me?" she asked.

"Yes of course."

"Oh please. You left Boston for San Francisco after five months. You'd rather be alone than have us around to help you. You couldn't stand it here. You can tell me the truth."

"Then no, I don't miss you," I said.

She brought her hand to her forehead, her predictably dramatic gesture.

I laughed louder, now clapping my hands. We were watching reruns of her favorite TV mystery on her bed, eating dark chocolate truffles. It was past two in the morning. We'd already gone through two boxes in four episodes.

My son was sleeping on the living room sofa bed, waiting for me to lie down beside him. He was at the age that's old enough to fall asleep alone but young enough to long for my warmth. We visited my extended family every winter break. Yesterday and today we stayed with Bubbe in Lynn, north of Boston. Tomorrow we would leave to see my father-in-law and his wife even farther north, by New Hampshire.

"Will you miss me tomorrow?" she asked.

"Let me think about it."

"You've had eight years to answer this question. How much more time do you need?"

"Until you are gone."

"Are you saying until I'm dead?"

"Yes."

"How dare you! I'm going to have to teach you how to be polite."

"No, I'd rather stay honest," I said, holding back my smile.

"Come. Give me a hug." She beckoned me, so I put my arms around her and tapped her back. "No no no, that is not a hug. Don't pat me. I am not your dog. Keep your arms in one place, rest your head on my shoulder, and stay still, for five seconds. Hug me like you love me."

"I can't," I said.

"Why? Don't you love me? Not even a little?"

"It's not that. I can't hug like you said."

"How long have you been in this family?"

"All right," I said, and I put my arms around her once more, and stayed still, my fingers spread on her back. She was wearing a nightgown made of thin cotton, and I could feel her sagging skin between my fingers. She was hugging me just the way I was hugging her. Her hair tickled my cheek and I heard 1920s jazz, a cornet solo, coming from the TV. I didn't know if I should close my eyes or where I was supposed to look.

"There," she said as she moved away. "See, I told you, it's not that hard."

"You know what," I said. "We don't have 'hug' in our language either."

"No 'I miss you' and no hugs. How do you know love?"

"We read the air," I said.

———

I see the father in the corner of my right eye every day at my son's elementary school as parents and students gather for morning exercise assembly. He has twins, one who stays next to him until the bell goes off and the other who walks by me, and that's how I know that the father has arrived. I knew his wife too; she died a year ago: cancer. I remember seeing her at the kids' soccer games. On kickoff day, she wore a knit cap. It was September, Indian summer; the temperature had hit eighty degrees. I noticed her eyebrows were too perfectly drawn yet slightly out of place, and her eyes, to me, seemed bare and somehow incomplete. She was extremely pale, to the point that I could see green veins just below her skin.

"Her cancer came back," a mother next to me whispered.

I didn't know she'd had cancer before. Our kids weren't in the same class.

As the soccer season moved on, her health deteriorated, and by the middle of the season, she sat in a camping chair that they brought, wearing a ski jacket, the knit cap, and two scarves while the other parents wore lightweight sweatshirts. I carried a blanket with me just in case she needed one, but someone always stood by her, giving her a hot drink from a thermos. So I laid the blanket on the grass and watched my son play, alone.

Shortly after the soccer season ended, I received an email from one of the mothers telling me that Patty Langton had passed away, surrounded by her family, with an attached sign-up sheet for weekend dinner shifts to help Patty's husband. I didn't sign up. The shift was already filled five months in advance; besides, I knew the hardest time would be a year and a half after her death. The first year we are too busy adjusting to our new reality, emotionally and practically. The grieving comes after three years, four years, much later, like when we are in the car on the way to work after dropping the kids off at school; the tiny gaps in our lives, that's when we realize there is something wrong with us.

I don't talk to him. I just watch him doing jumping jacks with his boy from the corner of my eye. When the bell goes off, I merge into the crowd and walk behind the father, looking at two deep horizontal creases on his tanned neck. Then I do the same the next day. The boy passes me by. I catch the father and his other boy doing jumping jacks, find more wrinkles on his neck, and leave.

# The Death of the Fish

THE DAY AFTER ALEX'S FIFTH BIRTHDAY, HE ASKED ME IF HE COULD have a fish for his sixth birthday. I said yes. A boy his age changes his wishes every hour so I assumed he would change his mind by his next birthday. He not only remembered but also began writing about the fish in his school journal. It started with one simple line, "I want a fish." As his birthday neared, it turned into a story called "How to Teach Guitar to My Fish." Alex won a school writing contest with the story.

————

The weekend Alex turned six, we were at a pet store.

In less than five minutes, he spotted a fish and said, "I want this fish."

He pointed to a shiny blue body with a long, wide, and red tail. A sign read BETTA: SIAMESE FIGHTING FISH. The description said that if it stayed alone in a fishbowl, it would live for a long time without much care. Before my son could change his mind I placed the fish container in my basket. We walked around the store and chose a small fishbowl, marbles, water solution, fish food, and some decorations, and went to the cashier.

"I want to hold it," Alex said to the cashier, who was about to put the container into a plastic bag.

"Of course," she said and handed it to him.

Alex cradled the fish container the way he would hold a kitten.

"It is easy to take care of, right?" I asked.

"Oh yes. This is a fighting fish. They need to be alone in order to survive, but other than that all you need to do is be careful with the water. They like lukewarm water," the cashier said as she put the rest of our things into the bag.

His fish, named Coodybug, was placed in the center of the dining table. Inside the bowl, the fish seemed to love the single leafy plant very much. He often hid in its rolled-up leaves. Alex said that Coodybug was playing hide-and-seek with us.

Before Alex left for school, he said goodbye to the fish, and when he came home, he gave him five tiny nuggets. We watched the fish suck up the floating nuggets one by one like a vacuum while we ate afternoon snacks together.

After three weeks, the water was dirty so I suggested we change it. Alex carefully scooped up the fish with an empty yogurt container and dumped the rest of the dirty water into a sink. I cleaned the fishbowl with a brand-new sponge, then filled it with warm water. Alex dropped in exactly seven drops of water solution. We waited five minutes, then we put the fish back into the bowl. He happily splashed around for thirty seconds, then we saw him sinking to the bottom. I shook the bowl, but the fish was no longer scared of the shaking. He swayed right and left, with the water. *No way,* I thought. I rolled up my sleeve and put my hand into the bowl. The lukewarm water was not *luke* but warm.

"Is he dead?" Alex asked.

Looking at the poached fish in my palm, I groped for how to explain this to my son.

———

The summer he turned four, it was a baby blue flower. I cannot recall the type of plant, but Alex named it Fluffy. He often squatted on the ground, trying to smell Fluffy. He listened to my warning about touching the flower, "If you touch the flower it will die." The tip of his nose came so close to kissing the flower, but he had never tried to touch it. After a vacation to see my parents in Japan, we found Fluffy in the garden turned into a dried flower.

"Is it dead?" he asked.

I nodded, looking straight at him.

Alex and I buried Fluffy in the dirt there. We gave a short Buddhist prayer.

———

The first time we visited my parents' house in Japan was the fall before Alex turned two. My husband, Levi, had to work, so he stayed home in San Francisco. Levi, who couldn't stand for a day to go by without talking to us, did not call for three days. He had not answered the home phone, his business phone, or his cellphone, so I called my mother-in-law, and she called the police. This is how they found him, under the Impala. Back then a 1964 Chevy Impala, as big as a boat, occupied our garage. I'll never know what Levi was trying to do under the car. The jack slipped and the five-thousand-pound Chevy crushed his chest.

"He lost consciousness instantly. Within three minutes he was dead. He did not suffer," my mother-in-law told me at the airport, where his entire family waited for us to arrive back from Japan. After the autopsy, the medical examiner told us Levi was in no condition to be seen just then. Despite the suggestion, I pleaded, then went to see

Levi. I left Alex with my mother, who had flown to the U.S. with us for support.

The gray-walled hallway continued as far as I could see; then a cold metal door appeared in front of me: Room 4. I opened the door, and in the corner of the room, I saw a body covered with a white sheet. Except for the bruise on his left eyelid, he looked in good condition. He might have been sleeping, I thought. With my ring finger, I touched his cheek. He was cold. It was not the coldness that sinks into your bones and not the coldness that children bring after coming back in from a snowball fight. It was a coldness I could never warm.

I haven't found the words to describe this sensation, yet when I think about that moment, my now empty finger feels the chill.

———

"Even though he's a child, it's always better to tell the truth," my therapist told me, so I explained to Alex what had happened to his father. I even brought him to my therapist a few times. Alex loved the tiny figures in the sandbox so much that he wanted to take them home and refused to leave the office. The therapist gave him a red lollipop at the door. I asked her if it was some kind of medicine to ease his sadness. She said no. I licked it once just to be sure before I gave it to him.

———

"Alex, the water was too hot. I killed Coodybug. I am so sorry." I told the truth.

"Yeah . . ."

"You can be mad at me. You can scream at me or hit me. Anything."

"Okay," Alex said, looking at the fish in my palm.

"What do you want to do?"

"Return him to the water."

"The ocean?"

"In the toilet. That's what you do. I saw it in a movie."

We walked to the bathroom together and returned Coodybug to the water in the toilet and said a short prayer.

"Goodbye, Coodybug." We waved at him in the swirling waves.

"Are you sad? You know that you can be," I said.

He nodded.

"Let me read you a book." I held his cheeks in between my hands and kissed his forehead.

This brightened him up. "Yeah!" He jumped twice. Books always comforted him.

I brought a book my therapist had given him. We sat on my bed to read. The story was about a leaf on a tree losing his friend in winter, but gradually accepting the death of his friend and happily going back to the soil when it was his turn.

This was a beautiful story that I often read for myself after Alex went to bed. It told the virtue of life, the law of nature, the things we all go through; we were part of the big tree. I could believe it. I felt kinder to all humanity.

"Do you know my friend Sophia? She can touch her nose with her tongue," said Alex, stretching out his tongue as far as he could. He then fell on his back. His arms and legs spread nice and long, and he began to move his arms up and down.

"Look, mama!" he said.

He was making a snow angel on the sheets.

# My Father

MY FATHER IS A CITY WORKER WHO MANAGES THE ENTIRE SEWAGE system in Tokyo. According to my mother, he is the happiest man that she has ever known.

———

Once in a great while, when he was drunk though not enough to pass out, he would scribble in the air for a scratch pad and a pen. We bounced up and down because that meant he was going to draw. My younger brother and I were around three and six years old then.

"What do you want?" he'd ask, and I would say, "A koala!" and my brother would say, "No, a robot!" Then he drew a koala robot on a building which looked like a tree. After that, he asked for more paper but stopped asking us what we wanted. He just drew one animal after another as my mother sat next to him, ripping junk mail into quarters with a ruler to make scratch pads. A giraffe on a trampoline. A jaguar juggling three black balls. The three wise monkeys drinking beer in a hot tub served by dogs who were supposed to be guarding the shrine. Snakes who dressed up as dragons, saying, *It's not easy to pretend to be strong.* By the time he ran out of the scratch pads, we had a collage of animal cartoons. My brother and I made up stories that went with each drawing as my father smiled, showed his crooked teeth, lit a cigarette, and drank more sake.

"There is nothing he cannot draw," my mother said as she brought him another bottle of hot sake. I remember the dusty orange light shade above our living room, the smoky air, and my mother gazing at my father with her melting eyes.

"That's all for today," he would say, gathering his cartoons together before taking them to the trash can. And that was that. We went to bed.

———

When I told my father that the steam from the coffee cup looked like a ballerina dancing, he told me to write a poem.

———

We had no art in our house. Our house was too small to fill with luxuries. The single painting in the hallway had always been there, but I didn't notice it until I was in junior high school.

"Your father did it. He used to paint a lot," my mother told me.

A village in front of a mountain, the different shades of green, the red houses, and a river—typical of northern Japanese scenery—like a painting that I might see in the bathroom of a run-down restaurant. I couldn't say it was beautiful or memorable.

At the time, I was undecided about whether I should become a nuclear power plant worker, a guide dog trainer, or just quit living.

"Where are his other paintings?" I asked my mother.

"Gone. They took up too much space. We threw them away."

———

Twice I discovered my parents' old journals. Once, when I was twenty-five, I found my mother's with a list written to us: where she hid the code for the safe box, the life insurance company's phone number, and the address of the medical facility to donate her body to. The other time was right after high school. In the bathroom, a small blue notebook lay on the floor. If there was a hole in the wall, you'd look through it. If there was an unlabeled notebook, you'd open it. So I picked it up and opened it as my instinct pleased. In the journal, my father had written, *Day 1: I have failed the college exam two years in a row. It's cold outside. I am destined to wander and to paint, on this mountain. No job, no money, no love, just me and a pencil.* My father was twenty years old, alone on a cold mountain in winter. I closed the notebook and sat on the toilet seat. *Why is it here?* I thought about opening it again to make sure of what I'd read, that he was not born to be a sewage worker, but I didn't have the courage to hold that reality, so I pushed the journal to the side with my toes and counted to three hundred before I flushed the toilet.

In the living room, my father was holding a newspaper in one hand and with the other, pulling at his nose hairs.

———

I was suspended for a week from high school, ten days before my graduation. I didn't do anything wrong other than go get my driver's license without their permission. My teacher found out because I called her by mistake, thinking I was calling my piano teacher, and left a message saying that I had to miss a lesson to take the license exam. We had no more classes and only one practice day left for graduation ceremony; still, my teacher suspended me and assigned me to write a five-page essay expressing my regret. I was always a good student, a role model, and a teacher's pet, but in the end I'd turned into a terrible student. That night, while I stared at my tear-smudged letters on the paper, thinking there would be no future ahead of me, my father sat across from me and drank sake as usual. He stole one of the pages from me and drew a Japanese monkey, the classic remorseful monkey, its face looking halfway down, its hands on its knees, and its shoulders slouched as if under the weight of a large sack of rice.

"The key to survival in this world is to *pretend* to be like this monkey," my father said and gave me a confident nod. He drained a cup of sake in one gulp and wrote the essay for me.

"Don't take this so seriously. Suspended before graduation! That's my girl! Copy my essay and give it to your teacher, she will be impressed."

———

I didn't tell my father when I found out I was pregnant and decided to marry Levi, a guy he'd never met, in the country he had never been to. I told my mother to tell my father and report back to me his reaction. Two weeks later, a letter arrived from home.

> *I don't care if he is Jewish or Muslim. I don't care if he is the President of the United States or a construction worker. As long as he is working and supports you and your baby and you are happy, I am happy for you.*
>
> > *Your father*

On the bottom of the letter, there was a picture of a sleeping baby in his mother's arms. For the first time, he drew my face.

———

I am on the bullet train from my best friend's town to my hometown. In my right hand, I hold a warm rice ball and in my left two ten-thousand-yen bills my friend has given to me. My son and I are visiting Japan for the first time since he was born. But I was away from my parents' house when my mother-in-law phoned my mother from America to tell me about Levi's accident.

According to my mother, my father is the happiest man she's ever known. In the last thirty-six years, he had solved all the problems of the entire sewage system in Tokyo, often with a hangover. His job never caused him stomach ulcers, cancer, or kidney stones. The job was as easy as combing his bald head, he told her.

The train stops and I hear the announcer calling out the name of my town. My parents and my son will be waiting at the entrance gate. Stepping onto the escalator, I imagine my father's face when he finds me in the crowd. I'll find a crack in the ground to trip over, right in front of him, to make him laugh, to make him forget why he is there, and to make him reach for me without us having to look into each other's eyes.

# Would You Tell Me What I Want?

MY MOTHER, BUBBE, AND I WERE SITTING ON THE RED COUCH, THE couch Levi's friend was going to take in two days. In two days, I'd be leaving this house for Boston, to live with Bubbe and my brother-in-law's family. We flew to Massachusetts with Levi's body, returned to San Francisco after the funeral, and now the house was packed and ready for foreclosure.

"We did it! The house is empty and clean. We deserve something for ourselves," Bubbe said. "Tell me, Kyoko, what do you want to do? What would make you happy?"

"I want to stay in San Francisco," I said.

"No, not that, but anything else. Anything. What do you *really* want?"

"Nothing," I said.

"Well, I'll tell you what *I* want. I want to go to see a fortune-teller. I want to see how happy we all will be, because you know we will. We just don't know how yet."

I told her that I knew of one on Ocean Avenue. This made her happy.

"How about you? What do you want, Masako?" she asked my mother, who was sitting on the edge of the sofa on the other side of her. I interpreted for my mother. My mother, who giggled with her hand to her mouth whenever Bubbe asked her something, stayed silent.

"She is asking you, Mother. What do you want?"

Suddenly, at the speed of light, my mother stood in front of me, screaming in Japanese, "All I want is for you to put on makeup! You never put on any makeup when Levi was still alive! Not even your eyebrows!" Then she began to sob, her body shaking uncontrollably.

My mother-in-law, who had rarely seen my mother speak, froze. In my peripheral vision, I saw Bubbe's eyes bouncing back and forth between my mother and me. I sent an unspoken begging sign to Bubbe with my eyes: *Help! My mother is going insane.*

Bubbe gave me the *I got your back. Bubbe knows best!* look, which I'd depended on so many times after Levi's death. Yes, she would know what to do with my mother.

Bubbe rose slowly and reached for my mother's hand and said, "Yes, I know, Masako, we all miss Levi, don't we?" then embraced my mother for a very long time.

———

I dropped onto my bed, bounced on it once, then landed. My black dress slowly fell over my thighs, and I felt a chill from the silky material. The chill continued to creep up my tailbone, my spine, and the back of my neck. Goosebumps chased the chill over my arms, and at the same time, the air conditioner expelled cold air, so I wrapped myself in the brand-new bedcover that my brother-in-law had bought me. The bed and the bedding set were gifts from him to make me feel I was a part of this family. My brother-in-law had moved his dead-weight vintage oak desk, white leather reading chaise, and his Civil War coin collection out of his library and replaced them with this bed and the crib set for my son. The chaise and desk were stacked haphazardly in the hallway and the coin collection in a plastic grocery bag tossed under the desk. He had not found the time to move his furniture into the basement. I wanted to cry and to be moved by his thoughtful gesture, but my body was too honest to produce any tears. I felt ashamed, so I thought about how I could punish myself. To stop eating his food could be one way to show my appreciation. I could also become his maid, scrubbing his toilets, taking his girls to violin lessons, or cooking for his family. But for now, I didn't even have the strength to get up, so I bit my tongue, pinched my inner thigh hard, and inhaled the toxic smell of the brand-new bedcover. But when I felt too much pain in my thigh, I let my bite go. I'd failed to even make myself bleed.

I glanced at the clock. In twenty minutes, my mother-in-law would come get us, me and my mother, with Alex, and when she came, I would have to show up in front of hundreds of people.

My mother was standing in front of the bathroom mirror.

"You are lucky," my mother said, "everyone loves you."

From my bed, I saw her naked face in the mirror. She touched her skin to take a closer look at her age spots. She tried rubbing them off, then picking at them.

"No matter what you do, they won't go away. They're permanently stained," I told her.

She said she knew and opened her facial cream.

"You know why else you are lucky? Because you are still young," she said as she dabbed the cream on her cheeks, chin, the tip of her nose, and forehead. She scooped more cream, leaned closer to the mirror, and with a circular motion, rubbed it forcefully into her face. Then she pulled out a case of concealer and, with a small brush, painted it over her spots. After that, she applied her foundation, first on her cheeks, the sides of her nose, eyelids, then chin and forehead. Her ritual, her flawless face comforted me just as they had twenty years ago when I used to watch her transformation in the mirror at home. I wanted to keep following her, but my vision began to blur. My tears ran and ran, creating a stream from one of my eyes to my nose. When my nose couldn't hold my tears any longer, they traveled to my lips. I licked the salty liquid. The tears from my other eye stopped nowhere. They just ran straight down and wet my bedcover.

"Did you already put your makeup on?" my mother asked me as she was coming out of the bathroom.

I shook my head.

"Hurry up, Bubbe will come to get us soon."

I shook my head again.

"It's your husband's funeral. Everyone will come to say something to you, so you must look nice."

"I don't care."

"All right then, just do your eyebrows. You look like a ghost with your thin eyebrows."

"What does it have to do with Levi? Only you'll notice that."

I got up to leave the room. Then my mother, a petite Japanese woman, pushed me back onto the bed. I fell backward and saw the chandelier sparkling on the ceiling. Just as I decided to give up on my life, she pulled my arms, forcing me to sit up, and sat on my lap.

"It's not for anyone. This is not for Levi or me. Okay?" she said and took out her facial cream and began smearing it on my face. The cream dissolved into my tears. My mother wiped them off with tissues and put the cream back on, and when it dissolved again, she wiped my face and applied it yet another time. I sat like a soulless doll. She wiped and applied and wiped and applied until she won over my tears.

"This is not for him. He is not my daughter." *My daughter, my daughter,* she repeated and pressed powder onto my face. "Trust me, you'll feel better once you have makeup on. I know it."

———

"Tell me the truth. Do you like classic cars?" Levi asked. We were on the way to a car show.

I answered, "Not really."

"Then let's do something you like. What do you *really* want?"

"This is what I want to do, sit next to you in our Falcon. I don't care where we go. That's all I want," I said.

He looked at me like I'd said something funny. His sunglasses hid his eyes, but I saw his eyebrows come together, his mouth forming a small O, and his head cocked to the side. I rubbed his knee and smiled. I wanted to scream to the world, *Show me someone who is luckier!*

He turned on the ignition and started singing along with a song on the radio. I got the feeling that something exciting was about to happen. I laughed, beating the dashboard like a drum. I loved the way he arched his back when he tried to hit a high note. The noise never bothered Alex. He was six months old, still a newborn, and I was twenty-six, a newlywed.

# My Jewish Genie

WE HEADED TO CAPE COD BECAUSE WE HEARD THERE WERE SURF spots and fortune-tellers. A snowy Christmas morning, the traffic was sparse and the few drivers that were on the highway passed us honking at my bubbe's slow-driving car. We didn't care though. We were first-year mourners. We could do whatever we wanted.

I wasn't Jewish like my bubbe. I wasn't even American. I was Japanese, but according to Bubbe, I *was* Jewish in my past life.

*How else to explain our tight sisterhood?* she said to me once.

*We aren't sisters. We are in-laws, forced to bond by loss, not by choice,* I told her.

Since my real target was dead already, I wished, at least, that my meanness could break his mother.

She'd say, *Then bless him, he brought us together.*

"Here, have some." While my bubbe drove, she grabbed some Utz's chips and placed them on my lap. "They're good for you, low in sodium. Only the best for my daughter-in-law."

I said thank you, but instead of chips I picked skin at the side of my thumb and ate it. If I put something in my mouth besides my skin, it was either Alex's leftovers or the burnt edge of a kugel that even my brother-in-law's dog walked away from without sniffing. I loved Bubbe's kugel. When I used to eat, I ate a plate full of it topped with whipped cream and everyone laughed at me because no one in the family had ever eaten kugel with whipped cream. "I'm starting a new tradition," I said and laughed. This was back when I still could laugh until I made myself cry. I had stopped laughing, eating, and crying three months before, when Alex and I moved in with my brother-in-law's family.

The phone rang and I grabbed a pen and a clipboard.

"Hello, this is Neighbors' Hardware," I answered.

A man, always a man, yelled at me over the phone, *Where are my screws? I'm reporting you to the Better Business Bureau!*

My body cringed.

"I am so sorry. As soon as it ships, I will let you know," I said.

*A girl answered the phone the other day. She couldn't even make out a sentence. What are you? Two Chinese girls trying to scam me? You better cancel my order. Regardless, I'm reporting this to the Better Business Bureau!*

"Yes, you are absolutely right. We can—we certainly can cancel your order," I said. The man continued to yell at me and I kept bowing over the phone. "I apologies for the delay. The truth is that the owner of this company was killed in an accident, so we are just trying to figure things out."

His voice changed its tone, now quieter. After one last bow, I ended the call and tossed the phone onto the dashboard.

"You were perfect, like you've owned the company for years," Bubbe said.

"He called me a girl."

"Because he's a schmuck! What did he order?"

"A box of screws."

"That's all? See, I told you, he is a schmuck."

The phone rang again.

"Kyoko, don't answer. For Christ's sake, it's Christmas."

I repeated the same lines to the caller, another man.

"Another screws," I said as I hung up.

"Another schmuck. Kyoko, give me the phone." Bubbe grabbed the phone from me, turned the power off, and shoved it in the glove compartment.

I sank deep into my seat. The chips rustled down to the floor.

"Have some chocolate. It's seventy-two percent cacao. Good for your heart." Bubbe took several pieces of candy from her pocket and placed them on my lap. Now I had chips by my feet and candy on my lap. I pulled a pair of tweezers out of Alex's diaper bag, picked my hangnail, and ate it.

Bubbe rubbed my knee and said, "As long as we have each other, we'll be okay."

Leaning on the window, I stared at Bubbe for a second, then looked away. Bubbe didn't see me. Her eyes were on the road; as always, she focused on moving forward.

I stretched my arm to Alex in the backseat and squeezed his feet. He was almost two, cute and quiet if the car kept moving.

I hadn't surfed in San Francisco—though I'd wanted to—and Bubbe had already tried a psychic on Ocean Ave in San Francisco. Why were we doing this now, in Massachusetts? We were first-year mourners, we didn't need a reason.

"I've decided," Bubbe declared. "Today is our day. No Zaydeh, no Levi, no Ben, and no Neighbors' Hardware. Men, they only give us trouble. Today is a day for Bubbe and Kyoko."

"And Alex?" I asked.

"We schlep him along with us but no, it's not his day. Every day is Alex's day. Today is just for us. We can eat whatever we want: ice cream, Chinese spareribs, sushi. We can say whatever we want to say: *schmuck, idiot, I love you.*"

"Can you turn the radio on, Bubbe?"

"Certainly, I can. I can turn on the radio for you. I can even dance for you. People think I can't dance. Ha! What do they know! I'm the only one who's got rhythm in this family. Watch me, here comes the dancing queen."

Bubbe began to jiggle, her head bobbing up and down, swaying left and right.

"Okay, what else, Kyoko? I'm your Genie but not a stingy one like from *Aladdin.* I'm a Jewish Genie. I can grant you more than three wishes."

"I want to go." I spoke to the window. "Alex is so small, he won't know the difference. Nothing will change even if I'm gone."

Bubbe held my hand. I didn't push her hand away but didn't hold it back either.

"In Yiddish," Bubbe said, "we say *bashert.* It means 'it's meant to be.' You are meant to live. I lost my son but gained a daughter. I love you."

"Thank you," I said.

"*I love you too, Bubbe,* is what you should say."

A smile grew on my lips.

"Now it's my turn to say what I want: Kyoko, you're my Jewish Japanese Genie. I want to see a fortune-teller who can tell me about my love life. I want a man who can buy me jewelry and take *us* to a Chinese restaurant whenever I want."

I smiled a little bit more.

"Here comes my third wish, my Jewish Genie," I said. "I wish to stop at Levi's."

"Of course. Your wish is granted."

According to my bubbe, my brother-in-law was the best baby you could hope to have. He sat, ate, slept, and only cried when he was hungry. If Bubbe left him in the crib, he would lay there without a peep as his eyes followed the mobile spinning along with the sounds of "Rock-a-Bye Baby" until it stopped. He would sit on a blanket and watch Bubbe hang sheets outside. He would stay in his high chair, sucking a pickle while Bubbe cooked. If having a baby was this easy, why not have another one? Bubbe and Zaydeh decided. Fifteen months after Ben was born, my husband, Levi, came into the family. What Bubbe and Zaydeh didn't expect was to have a baby who could move faster than his parents. By seven months old, Levi could run across the room while Ben still toddled. Once Levi mastered running, he climbed out of his crib, then climbed into his brother's crib to sleep or play. According to Bubbe, Levi was the one who taught his brother how to open and get into the clothes dryer.

When Levi turned six, Paula and Laura were born. The two brothers used to push each of the girls in a stroller. "Bet you can't beat me," one of the brothers would say and race down their slanted driveway like in a sled dog race. Ben won twice with Paula in her stroller. Levi won the rest of the time until Laura broke her nose. When Laura tells the story, touching her bent nose, her face blooms and it always ends with her saying, "I have wild brothers who love me dearly."

By age six, Ben wore collared shirts and ties, and Levi wore a T-shirt and engine-oil-stained jeans. At age thirteen, Ben's focus was on investing

his Bar Mitzvah money, and that same year, Levi had thirteen school de-
tentions. But, as Bubbe said, they were inseparable. In the morning, they
would compete to see who could eat the most Froot Loops in thirty seconds, and in the afternoon, they rode their bikes to the junkyard. While
Ben studied inside an abandoned car, Levi dug for car parts.

The two brothers lived together in Sharon for ten years. At age
twenty, they bought a house, across from their synagogue, and lived
there until Levi moved to San Francisco. I wonder, if Levi had stayed
in Sharon, would the brothers still be eating Froot Loops for breakfast
and dinner, Ben in his tailored suit and Levi in a T-shirt and jeans. Ben
would throw a wet Froot Loop at Levi and laugh while they watched
*Star Trek.*

Levi returned to the town, to Sharon Memorial Park, a few months
ago, in September, cold and dead.

I wonder, if Levi had returned alive, perhaps Ben would not have
decided to go to Iraq. Levi could have found a hundred reasons to stop
him. If talking didn't work, he would find a way to get on the airplane
with him. If Levi had lived, Bubbe wouldn't even need to prepare for
another possible loss. Yes, this was her *bashert*. This was meant to be.
As chatty as she was, she didn't mention this, and I didn't dare to
ask her.

Bubbe took exit 23A, turned left, then took another left on Ded-
ham Street to Sharon Memorial Park. In Jewish cemeteries, there are
no gravestones, only plaques. If you didn't know, you'd think it was a
park, and that's the way they liked it. Bubbe told me once, *We've expe-
rienced enough attacks. At least let us rest in peace.*

"Would you leave a rock for Levi from me? It's too icy for me to get
a grip on my cane," Bubbe said.

There was no plaque on his grave yet, only a small red flag sticking out of the snow. I stood by him for a while, then kicked him through the ground.

"You don't deserve stones. You don't even deserve to die," I said.

My white breath came out at the same rhythm as my kicks.

"Death is a privilege, you know. It's a privilege!" I told him.

From Sharon, Bubbe and I drove to the fortune-teller's house. The house wasn't on the cute tourist street that I imagined people came to on a summer vacation. It was surrounded by a liquor store, a cash advance and loan place, and an adult toy store. The neon sign read, SPYCHIC and beneath the dull blinking sign, there was a scrawled note: *Best Psychic Reading and Bail Bonds on the Cape.* The Scotch tape on the piece of paper had yellowed and collected dust around the edges. *Spychic* stood behind a barred door.

"This is it!" Bubbe said. "This is the one my friend told me about."

"Are you sure you want to go in? It says bail bond. It doesn't seem safe here." I tightened my grip on Alex's baby carrier. I was ready to run away without Bubbe.

"Kyoko, trust me. Real psychics always hide where you least expect. Besides, there is nothing safer than inside a bail bondsman's office."

I couldn't really understand her logic, but I let it go and we pressed the doorbell.

A middle-aged man with chest hair flowing from his white tank top opened the door. He didn't carry a baton. In fact, he wore elastic-waist pants, no belt.

"What do you want, to bail someone or a candle?"

"Psychic," said Bubbe.

"Customers!" the man shouted to no one in particular, then went up a staircase. From a half-open door, I saw a boy, about Alex's age, in a huge playpen staring blankly at a TV screen hanging on the wall. The light from the TV illuminated the boy's face in a muted blue and purple glow.

"There is a bad aura, Bubbe. This is a depressing place. And *I'm* saying it's depressing, so it must be really depressing," I whispered into her ear.

"Don't worry, Bubbe knows best," she whispered back.

We went in.

I released Alex from his baby carrier. He immediately walked over to the playpen and stood by to keep the boy inside it company. Both of them were mesmerized by the talking purple dinosaur on the muted TV. Bubbe and I took a seat on the sofa. The room smelled like cat pee and wet diaper.

"Hello? Hello? Are you there?" A woman like the old lady from the "young old woman" optical illusion came downstairs, holding the railing in one hand and sliding the other along the wall as though she were waiting for each step to appear before she went down. The way she took the steps and the way she spoke reminded me of my grandfather who was blind, so I knew she couldn't see well.

"I'm Ethel, and this is my daughter and my grandson," Bubbe said.

"Ethel . . .yes, yes, I was expecting you! My name is Maria. Shall we begin?"

Yes, Bubbe said. Come this way, the fortune-teller said, and they went into the small room behind the playpen, which appeared to have been a walk-in closet in another life. There wasn't a door, just a curtain.

"Before we start, let me explain how my power works," the fortune-teller said to Bubbe as she closed the curtain.

Now I was left alone with two toddlers, who were fascinated by a psychedelic dinosaur.

I opened the book that I had brought with me, a grief counseling book written by a therapist who studied Buddhist psychology in Colorado. Even though I had been studying psychology before I became a mother, I didn't understand at all what this therapist was saying. He made sense. His wisdom sounded useful, but my emotion didn't align. Where did my intelligence go?

I used to have a dream. I thought that the day after the doctor yanked out the person inside my belly I'd go back to school and Levi could feed the baby formula or whatever. I was ready to be separated from my child, at least in my head. Yet when I saw a small creature that couldn't even figure out where his body ended and mine started, I quit school. *Yes, you are here and I'm here.* My career, knowledge, sleep—all my wants rinsed away with my placenta. I lost a part of me with the arrival of my son, and that was a good thing.

Becoming a mother was my *bashert*—my fate. But *bashert* didn't guarantee financial security. *Here you go, good luck. Bashert* dropped me and my son, naked, in the Colosseum with a starving lion. I would be happy to be eaten if it was just me. But I'd fight to keep my son alive. The betrayal I felt from Levi. Neighbors' Hardware, solely run by him, was overrun by debt and cancellation orders, and the creditors chased him for money. It was only a matter of time before the company collapsed. Death was a privilege and Levi took even that away from me.

"Your daughter-in-law?"

Suddenly I heard the fortune-teller's voice. I awoke with the sensation that time had skipped a little. I must have fallen asleep. Alex? Immediately turning to the playpen, I found both the boys still glued to the TV. It had been about twenty minutes since Bubbe's session started, I thought, looking at the clock on the wall.

"Your daughter-in-law? Hmm, Ethel, you had a loss recently . . . someone very important."

The more I tried not to pay attention, the clearer their conversation got.

"Yes. My other son," Bubbe said in her usual clear voice.

"Ah, the daughter-in-law that you are talking about was his wife, correct? Hmmm, I don't trust her. Your son wasn't happy with her. I see your son is still here. He wants to tell me . . . Wait! He is saying, *I love you, Mom.*"

"No, no. That is not it," Bubbe said, in a voice louder than her previous response.

"Yes, he is still here!" the fortune-teller said. "But your daughter-in-law . . . yes, I wouldn't trust her. She carries bad karma."

I imagined the fortune-teller confidently nodding her head.

"I know my son is still here! What I want to know is if my daughter-in-law will find love again. I want her to be happy," Bubbe said.

*My happiness?*

"Happiness for your daughter-in-law? Let me see," the fortune-teller said as if she used her telepathic power to tune into my inner voice. Now, she must be tracing Bubbe's palm lines with her middle finger. This time, though, she'd do so carefully. A good long five minutes had passed. "I feel cold energy from her, your daughter-in-law. It's overwhelming. Your warm energy won't win over her coldness," she said. "But it can be warmed with *my* prayer and *my* candle. This is how she can find her happiness. The candle is a hundred and ten dollars, but for you, my friend, a hundred dollars."

"Thank you but no thank you," Bubbe said.

I heard her pulling out her chair.

I quickly closed my eyes, pressing my face onto the damp,

moldy-smelling cushion. When the curtain opened, I lifted my head and yawned.

"Did you hear our conversation?" Bubbe asked me.

"No, I think I fell asleep."

"Good. We're done. We can go to the beach now."

"It hasn't even been a half hour."

"I said I'm done."

Bubbe handed two twenty-dollar bills to the fortune-teller. I grabbed Alex quickly and hung Bubbe's cane on my arm. She took my arm and slowly we walked out the door.

"Here is the beach. Go get a good-looking surfer, Kyoko, hopefully he's rich."

Bubbe parked at the beach. She had been quiet since we left Spychic.

"Bubbe, I hate your son."

Bubbe's face stiffened, her eyes scanned me from my head to my waist and back. Her chest expanded and deflated with her sigh, then expanded again and there she held her breath. I knew she was about to say something. The fortune-teller was right. I was not a good daughter-in-law. And I didn't care. We didn't share the same grief. Hers came from the past and mine from the future. She was his mother, and we were strangers. We didn't understand each other. I owed her nothing.

"Do you love your son?" Bubbe said.

I nodded.

"Good. I love my son too, but I hate your husband too. He left you."

I clung onto her and said, "I want to go home, to San Francisco."

I had more to say, more to ask her, but I said nothing more.

"Umi, umi," Alex screamed and banged the window for the ocean.

A noise of protest—he didn't like when the car stopped. I gently pushed Bubbe off me to take him out of the car seat.

"It's our day. He can wait." She pulled me back and held me tighter. "Your wish is granted, Kyoko. I'm your Jewish Genie, remember? I'm not stingy like the one in *Aladdin*. I can't tell you how, but trust me, you will go back to San Francisco because I say so."

Alex's shoe hit my head.

"Right," I said.

None of our problems were resolved. My husband was dead. His company was going bankrupt, and I didn't know how to support myself in that expensive city. As for Bubbe, her son was dead, another one could be . . . and she had a daughter-in-law who carried bad karma.

"Now, let me tell you what Maria told me about the man of my future in her *closet*. You wouldn't believe what's waiting ahead for this gorgeous sixty-two-year-old woman. It's quite exciting."

"UUUUUMIIIIIII!" Alex screamed again. He could wait another five minutes while Bubbe finished her made-up story about her soul mate. We were first-year mourners. We were going to do whatever we wanted.

渦 (*uzu*):
vortex

# I'll Miss You at Your Funeral

THE CONDO THAT MY PARENTS BOUGHT WAS BUILT IN THE EARLY eighties, at the height of Japan's economic growth. Twenty-four plain white five-story buildings, the symbol of Japanese dreams, shot to the sky like bamboo; *only forty minutes from Tokyo, a perfect place to raise children*. It was built for families whose fathers worked in Tokyo but couldn't afford to live there.

Inside the complex there were two parks, a tennis court, daycare, and, who knows why, a private detective's office. It was an hour and twenty minutes to Tokyo by bus and train, but it was indeed the perfect place to raise a child.

We had three bedrooms. One we called the Tatami Room. It was next to our living dining room. From the ages of three to eleven I slept with my mother and little brother in the Tatami Room. We each had our own pillow and blanket but no space for three futon mattresses, so three of us shared two. Three sliding paper doors divided the living dining room and the Tatami Room, and my mother closed them at eight-thirty for our bedtime. In the morning, my brother and I folded the futon we shared into thirds, like a pastry sheet, and after we left for school my mother hung the futons on the veranda until 3:00 P.M. A gift from nature, collected by my mother, was given to her children every night. If we tried hard enough, we could breathe in the remnants of sunlight through the warmed futon as we lay on it at night.

During the day, the Tatami Room turned into my mother's workshop. She burred the edges of the caps of permanent markers to earn 0.1 yen per cap. I used to enjoy helping her after school when I had no plans with my friends.

There was also my mother's triptych-mirror dressing table. I remember watching her put on her makeup carefully and check her combed hair from every angle just to go to a grocery store by our condo. After she left, I would sit in front of the mirrors and dab her facial cream on my face. I wasn't a big fan of the taste of her lipstick, so I applied my cherry-flavored lip balm instead. I got close to the middle mirror and held the two side panels of the mirror close to my face. I was entranced by a lot of beautiful *mes* smiling.

My father slept in another tatami bedroom, which was in the north corner of the house. My brother and I were kind of scared of the room. We called it the Ghost Room. The Ghost Room was cold and dark, and a mysterious hissing sound could be heard from the condo next door, which was vacant at the time. During the day, between 4:00 and 5:00 P.M., the room functioned as my brother's study room. He spent the least amount of time avoiding the ghosts. As a result, my brother developed a keen power of concentration. Even later, when he took over the room, he didn't spend more than an hour a day studying. The four of us still joke, "This is how he got into the best college in Japan: the Ghost. That forced him to find a strategy to learn practically."

My brother, who was three years younger than me, slept with my mother until he was in fifth grade. Then my parents gave him the Ghost Room. My brother gladly inherited the room from my father. There weren't any ghosts anymore. A young couple with triplets moved

in next door, and the authentic screams and laughter of children comforted him to sleep.

The third bedroom, where no one slept, was called the Western
Style because it was carpeted. I used that room to do my homework.
Two dull-gray metal bookshelves lined the walls. My father's first edi-
tions of manga, which he'd collected as a teenager, were jam-packed
in both bookcases, leaving no room for my books.

For my eleventh birthday, I asked my parents to give me the Western Style. For some reason, we believed laying a futon on a carpet
brought bedbugs, so they bought a black loft bed from a department
store catalog and my father assembled it for me. The four of us took
a trip to Tokyo to find a wardrobe closet. I chose one I imagined the
British royal family might have. I hung my uniforms and overcoat in
the right side of the closet, and my mother hung my father's suits in
the left. In the morning, my mother entered my room while I was
still asleep to prepare my father's suits. On weekend mornings, my
father opened my door unannounced to get his manga. I didn't mind
though. The Western Style was now called Kyoko's room, and I was
surrounded by my bed, desk, and the British royal wardrobe closet.

Each time I returned home from America, I found my father's
belongings in my room, another bookshelf, plastic airplane models,
electric shavers. My wardrobe no longer smelled of my cheap teen
body spray but rather of an old man's cigarettes. He also took over the
drawers of my desk for his sketchbooks and paints. My mother told me
he slept in my room now.

In a way, none of us owned a bedroom. The oshiire in the Ghost
Room was used to store family seasonal goods: camping gear, ski wear,
and a plastic Christmas tree. Our childhood photo album was in my
mother's kimono bureau in the Tatami Room. When I was eighteen,

I found a box of condoms in the bureau while I was looking for my yukata. It was unopened and had been expired for ten years. Come to think of it, I have no recollection of where my parents slept in those five years when my brother and I both had our own rooms. It had to be the Tatami Room, but I cannot remember them sleeping together.

My father was fond of order and was methodical. He often told my mother how to grill fish without making a mess. He monitored us every time we picked up food with our chopsticks. "Don't grab too much. Don't stab your food." He was careful of himself too; if he dripped soy sauce on the table, he slapped his cheek hard enough to turn red.

Once a month, the four of us took a family trip. He knew that one day we'd leave the house and start our own families. He wanted to make memories. My loving father had great intentions. For our weekend outings he wrote down the schedule by the minute. The day trip usually happened on Sunday, but for my mother it started on Saturday afternoon because she had to call the train company to confirm each schedule and answer my father's questions: *What are we going to make for a lunch box? Did Daichi and Kyoko pack their snacks? Don't we need to buy more pocket tissues?* If we were late for the train because my brother had to go to the bathroom, my father would become grumpy, not toward my brother but at my mother for not taking him to the bathroom before we left. I tried to squeeze every drop from my body two minutes before my father's schedule started so I could save my mother from my father's silent accusation. We felt like we were walking a tightrope once a month. So long as we remained on the rope, my mother was safe.

Luckily, on weekdays, he was often out drinking with his friends. The nights he was out, the three of us would occasionally go out to eat. On the way to the restaurant, my brother and I each held my mother's hands, and, swinging our arms, we sang songs that were popular at the time.

When my father was sober, he read history books while he kept the history program on. But when he was drunk, he talked about Japanese artists from the 1800s.

"The small number of westerners who were able to visit Japan brought back pottery, and because Hokusai's painting was wood printing, there were so many of his works that pottery makers wrapped pottery in his pictures. That's how Van Gogh discovered Hokusai. It wasn't the shogun or samurai who exported the greatest art from Japan. It was *us,* the people," said my father proudly, pointing at himself.

He taught us not just to believe what our history class taught us. "It's like a custom-made jigsaw puzzle," he said—in order to really understand, we would have to read all kinds of books by different authors, especially books about how ordinary people lived. "Then *you* decide, *you* put the history together," he said.

It was very rare that my father could make it to ten cups. Most of the time, he passed out after seven. At the fifth cup, he became overly affectionate with my mother, who was glued to the TV, crawled behind her, and began clinging to her.

"Stop touching me!" she yelled and elbowed him.

"Please. I want you. I cannot live without you. I love you," my father would say. Then he made fish lips, aiming toward my mother's neck.

My mother wrestled away from my father's embrace and hit his back with her fists.

"Get away from me!" my mother would shout, and that was the sign. We must fight with my father, a.k.a. Mr. Evil Hand. We burst out from our futon and made a dramatic entrance like an American cartoon hero would do. My brother and I sat astride my father's back. We hit him and kicked him with our heels as hard as we could. "Ouch!" he'd say and rub the area where one of us had given him a particularly painful shot, but his eyes were still on my mother. We were laughing, and my father never got mad at us no matter how hard we hit, kicked, and bit. My mother was serious, so was my father, but for us it was a game. Those nights they didn't care if we stayed up late. They were focused on something more important—my father after my mother's love, and my mother after her solitude.

Eventually my father's arms went limp, and he began to snore.

"He is so annoying," she said to herself, then moved his arms to the side and peacefully went back to her TV program. My brother and I retreated to the next room and buried ourselves under our blankets.

I cannot recall that my parents ever kissed, hugged, or even touched to remove lint from the other's shoulder. They held my brother's and my hands, kissed and hugged us all the time until we grew too old. But they didn't touch each other. Even when I lost Levi they hugged me, but they didn't hug one another.

I'm pretty sure that my father didn't have a mistress or lover in his life. Not only could he not afford one, but also all he wanted was my mother's love, no one else's. I couldn't count on his promises while he was drunk, but I believed what he said to my mother. *I cannot live without you.*

Every yen he made went directly to their joint account, and my mother managed the money. As long as he received his monthly allowance from her and there was sake and my mother waiting for him at home, he did not care how the money was spent. My mother didn't complain about how much my father made just as my father didn't complain about how much his allowance was. My mother had to smooth the edges of the permanent marker caps for 0.1 yen per cap, sew labels on the back of men's ties, and run up and down stairs to deliver the real estate ads to each mailbox in our twenty-four condo buildings three days a week. All my friends chatted with their crushes on the cordless phones in their rooms, while I had to stand in the living room, in front of my family, whispering into the black rotary phone. I was aware that we were not poor, but we were poorer than my friends who lived in the same condo complex.

Yet we were happy. I knew and felt we were. My mother sat across from us as we talked about our day while we ate our three o'clock snack. My father often brought us back cream puffs whether he was drunk or not. We took a three-day ski trip every winter to my father's friend's cabin. Even under my father's neurotic directions, we were so excited that we laid out our next-day outfits by our futon the night before the trip.

Once my mother and I were talking about my father's semiretirement party at work.

"They tell me, 'Masako-san, your husband is like a kid; his eyes are always shining with enthusiasm. He is not after status or money. We love working with him and drinking with him. We are going to keep him. He doesn't have to do a thing; he just needs to come to the office and be with us!' You see, Kyoko. That's your father. I want you to donate my body for medical use so you can save your money and time. No funeral for me. But we must have a funeral for your father. So many people love him and will miss him."

Then, she pulled a tissue box close to her. "I've never met someone who is so simpleminded and free from avarice. This man has not changed since I married him."

We took turns pulling out tissues as we cried fantasizing about my father's funeral.

My mother had the rare talent of finding a silver lining in any situation. Since Levi's death, she would often tell me, "Having a child with no husband is the best thing you could hope for in your life, if you can afford it. You don't have to think about what to feed him or look at his face, trying to read what he is grumpy about. If you don't want to cook, you can go out to eat with your child. When your child leaves home, all you need to do is to make enough money for yourself."

She was right. I didn't have to worry about Levi's cooking instructions or his love attacks. I could skip my shower or skimp some on grocery expenses to save up money for plane tickets to Japan as needed and no one would complain about my priorities. My son comes to my bed in the middle of night, and we sleep together. On the weekend, we go places when and wherever we feel like—no bathroom check, no schedule spreadsheet, no map.

But where are my tears when I think about my husband's funeral?

If I could, I would dig him up from his grave and stab his heart. I would stab his heart until it's minced. I would break all his bones to make him like a puppet. I would crush him into a ball and kick him back into his coffin. I would throw rocks at him, tree branches, the shovel that I dug him up with, and all the gifts he gave me. Then I would ask him, "Why did you have to love *me*?"

# Dreamland

EARLY ONE MORNING, ZAYDEH, MY FATHER-IN-LAW, WHO WAS A SEMI-retired pilot, called from the airport in Austin, Texas, saying that he was flying into San Francisco. Before I could tell him whether we would even be home, he hung up. Five hours later he was at our door, one small suitcase beside him.

He asked me to show him around the neighborhood, so each of us took one of Alex's hands. It was winter in San Francisco, seventy degrees and sunny.

"What a beautiful day! I believe it's snowing right now in Boston," Zaydeh said.

The term "global warming" came to mind, but I swallowed it. My father-in-law didn't believe in global warming. He didn't believe in universal healthcare. And he was against immigrants coming to America even though I was a Japanese immigrant. As I tried thinking of something to talk about, I glanced at Alex's feet. My four-year-old son was doing his best to keep up with our pace. I asked Zaydeh if my husband also walked pigeon-toed when he was a child. He said no, Levi didn't, but he had legs as long and skinny as a giraffe's. That would be appealing to Japanese people, I said. He chuckled. Alex stopped walking and instead, folded his legs, like a monkey, so together my father-in-law and I held and swung him.

Alex continued his monkey pose, and although my arm was becoming tired, and I was beginning to worry that his arms might fall from their sockets, I didn't stop, neither did my father-in-law.

He told me that a small airport near his town was looking for a Japanese customer service agent and that I could make a great life there. I nodded and said it sounded like a great job.

The sun was beginning to set, and the air was getting colder and closing in. Eventually, we came to the house my husband used to own. My father-in-law stopped and looked up. I looked up too. The lights were on, and from behind the sheer curtains, we could see that a boy of about ten years old lay on his bed, bouncing a ball off the wall.

"The only way for me to recover from this is to bring him back," my father-in-law said.

The boy behind the curtain got up and left, leaving the light on. My father-in-law stood there, a look of loneliness on his face, as he stared through the window at the empty room.

"Hold me, Zaydeh." Alex stretched his arms. Zaydeh lifted Alex and piggybacked. We headed back home. I watched the two of them as I walked two steps behind.

———

For nearly eight years, my father-in-law has been fighting with the town he lives in over wanting to purchase the property behind his house. It was his dream, he said, to build a house for each of his children and live as one big happy family. I was moved by his idea, so I told the first person I encountered after hearing this.

"Who would want to live with him?" Paula my sister-in-law said, presenting her empty hands in front of her as if to emphasize her point.

"I don't know," I said.

"Exactly," Laura said. The twins gave me a half smile and half frown and went to chase their kids.

––––––

Every Christmas Day, at Zaydeh's house, Alex unwrapped all his gifts and stacked them like a tower. The tower came to just above his chin no matter how tall he grew, and it never failed to make him smile.

"But we're Jewish!" my mother-in-law, who had divorced Zaydeh thirty years ago, said as she looked at the picture of Alex standing next to the world's tallest stack of gifts, the Christmas tree in the background. "And Zaydeh *is* still Jewish!" she added with her hand dramatically on her forehead like she'd gotten an acute fever. This happened every December 30, at Alice's Chinese restaurant, with red-colored pork spareribs and sweet duck sauce.

Deep down in his heart, the gifts were only secondary to Alex. I knew that, because every Christmas Eve, in his bed, he spent his last waking moments raising his fingers one by one and naming all his nine cousins and how old each had become. Two families and three grandkids from Zaydeh's new wife's side, four families and seven grandkids from his side—for a family of two, having more people than his fingers could account for was what excited Alex the most. Zaydeh didn't care about his Christmas gifts either, he didn't care about them even if they were called Hanukkah gifts. Just like Alex, he was only truly excited about having his children, his grandkids, and me in his house.

Christmas dinner started at six o'clock, but he always told his kids to come at four-thirty. Around four-fifty, Zaydeh would flip cushions on the couch. One year's worth of dust danced in the living room while his wife, in between sneezes, yelled at him to stop as she covered her mouth with her elbow, trying not to spray on her mashed potatoes.

What did this ritual have to do with his children's visit? Maybe nothing, except to give him something to distract himself from his excitement or disappointment. At five-fifteen, when the house began to smell like turkey, his wife's side of the family showed up. They brought the cold air in from the outside, and the smells of their own houses as well. Zaydeh would go out to work in his front yard at five-thirty. I wiped the foggy window and saw him pointlessly scraping dead leaves off the icy driveway, occasionally glancing at the front gate. Ten after six, his daughters' families arrived with their four kids. Each of them gave Zaydeh a hug and light kiss on his cheek, then moved on to Alex for a big squeeze. Almost every year one of the children, either Sophie or Isaac, would become upset and run to Zaydeh's wife because someone didn't let them use the bright red gun or they were simply hungry. This happened right around seven-fifteen, so we started dinner without my brother-in-law. We all sat down on cold folding chairs, and by the time the chairs warmed up, we'd finished the meal. Paula and Laura didn't even touch Zaydeh's Christmas dinner. With a cup of coffee in their hands, both stood behind Alex, side by side, combing his hair with their fingers, gazing at him tenderly. I imagined they were seeing a remnant of their brother in Alex's bird-nest hair, something only siblings would understand. When three different kinds of semi-homemade pies were lined up on the kitchen counter, my brother-in-law's family would show up. By then the house would be rattling and shaking with kids running up and down the hallway and the adults talking about football so that no one would notice his entrance, except my father-in-law, who had been waiting for his son to show up since five o'clock, or maybe the whole year. He could hear the car pulling up the driveway. He didn't open the door for his son. He just stood by the front door patiently waiting for him to enter.

There were twenty-one DVDs, covering the time from the birth of his first grandchild, now seventeen, to my son's first birthday. Zaydeh loved to play them after everyone had eaten their pie. "Everyone, come sit in the living room!" his wife would shout. The tone of her voice commanded attention, so all the adults crammed into the living room. As soon as the part with Alex's father appeared on the screen, my brother-in-law left for the basement, mentioning that he was getting a soda, followed by my sisters-in-law. When Zaydeh found himself surrounded by his wife, his wife's children, in-laws, me, and ten grandkids, he came to me and whispered, "Where did *everybody* go?"

———

My husband was ten when he drank a whole bottle of Robitussin. His brother caught him and called an ambulance. This turned out to be fortunate for my husband because it meant that he didn't need to work cleaning floors for his father's apartment building that weekend. It wasn't so much the cleaning he hated, it was Zaydeh's inspections that he feared. The crescent-moon-shaped scuff marks on the left toe of his father's work boots and his stained white gloves. *Not good enough, not quite good enough.* My husband would end the story smiling, explaining to me that the white gloves were probably already stained to teach him a lesson to never cheat on his father, but they only succeeded in teaching him what kind of father he never wanted to become.

———

My father-in-law bought everything in threes: soap, shampoo, cereal boxes, cans of condensed milk, cars, motorcycles, houses. One winter visit, I forgot to bring dental floss. I asked Zaydeh if I could have some. He brought me about seven inches of floss and assured me not to worry, that he could give me more tomorrow. I cut it in two halves to share with Alex, but as I tried to floss his teeth, it kept slipping off my fingers. After several attempts, I gave up and asked Zaydeh for more. He handed me a brand-new box of floss and waited until I cut two strings. Again, he assured me, in a friendly tone, not to worry, that there would be more for tomorrow.

———

For my husband's coffin, my father-in-law wanted a pine box, the traditional Jewish coffin, one that would eventually decompose along with my husband's body to be one with the earth. I liked the idea of returning to the earth, but it also happened to be the cheapest one in the catalog.

Paula and Laura rushed out the door, followed by my mother-in-law, my brother-in-law, Zaydeh, then the funeral director. Alone in the room with the coffin catalog, I turned the pages and studied them: the pink casket with rose stitches inside the velvet padding, an eighteen-gauge turquoise steel with copper trim, a poplar coffin with red velvet like the kind vampires slept in. After all these years, I can still recall those coffins in the catalog, but I have no recollection of the color of the coffin my husband ended up lying in. When my husband's family and the funeral director returned to the meeting room, they asked me which one I would want for my love. Six sets of eyes suddenly became one set of eyes. I couldn't decide, so I appointed the person who looked the saddest. My brother-in-law bought the most expensive coffin, one with cement insulation. With this one, my husband, they told me, would never disappear from the Earth.

———

I was back at Zaydeh's house for Christmas again. Without looking out the window, I could always tell when the snow piled up overnight on Zaydeh's yard, enough to make a snow fort. These mornings were much quieter than other mornings, as if the snow separated me from myself and the moment. For that moment I no longer knew where and who I was, and a strange peace began to take hold of me. I moved the curtain aside and saw the snowflakes joining each other on my windowsill, and far away in the haze, I could spot Zaydeh's dreamland, slowly sinking into the snow.

# In Winter, I Smile Under the Cold Rain

I AWOKE WITH WETNESS, THE WETNESS THAT LINGERED ON MY BODY. My nipples were erect, and when they brushed against my T-shirt, the bottom half of my body felt my past. In my past life, I have craved, indulged in, and held on to a man's skin for this sensation. I was a woman once.

Alex was sound asleep next to me, our legs wrapped together. I released him and gripped my thigh. I tried to stop my body from feeling it by tightening my grip. My heartbeat between my legs continued to throb next to him.

———

I keep the left side of my bed, the side closest to the bathroom, empty. Even at eight, Alex would still come to my bed after he went to the bathroom in the middle of the night, and when he came, he would wedge his feet in between my thighs. His face was smoother, more innocent than when he was awake. I used to wake at dawn, before the alarm, and take advantage of Alex sleeping. I would check his head for lice, his eyes for mucus, and count his freckles. I traced his forehead, his eyelids and nose, which was like a slide made of porcelain. My finger slipped over its bridge, again and again. Then, I would stroke his cheek with my own cheek, to the rhythm of his breathing, and recall summertime in Japan, the nights I watched my mother peeling the fuzzy skin from a white peach, the nectar running through between her fingers.

———

Every September 21, on the anniversary of my husband's death, I call my mother-in-law. I start our conversation with sniffling, just enough so she can hear me. Though my nose is clear, I manage to play a rhythmic sniffling duet with her. She then blows her nose three times and ends the conversation by saying, "Kyoko, it's time for you to find your happiness. You have sacrificed your life enough."

I tell her the truth, "Thank you, but I am happy the way I am."

My mother-in-law bursts into tears. As I hear her thanking me for giving her son the happiness he knew, I feel another layer of guilt thickening my heart.

———

On my husband's birthday, I buy a strawberry shortcake from the Italian bakery on Mission Street and invite over neighbors and some of his friends. They flip through the photo albums at the dining room table. The dim light illuminates them and their laughter with the story of my husband building a 1970 Nova engine in our garage. I sit apart from them, on a stool by the stove, scraping pancake batter from the counter surface while I wait for the water to boil. When my guests silently begin to poke at the remaining whipped cream on their slices of cake, I fear being asked how I am doing. Even more, I fear being hugged, being pressed against someone until I can feel the temperature of their body, because at that moment, they might notice that I am not empty, or worse, that I am content.

———

On the morning I found out that I was pregnant with Alex, Levi and I met at St. Francis. I told him not to worry, that everything was under control, the place for the abortion, the money, even the ride home. All taken care of. We had been together for only a few months, just long enough to leave my toothbrush at his place, nothing else.

"Hungry?" I said and waved to a waitress, smiling. I ordered coffee and a waffle.

Levi shook his head and sent her away. He didn't look at her, his eyes stayed on me the whole time.

"What should we watch tonight?" I asked.

He said, "Have you thought that I might want the baby? Have you never even thought that I want to marry you? You and me?"

The noise of the popular diner helped to fill the blank spaces in our conversation. I watched Levi unroll his napkin, laying the silverware out, putting it back into the napkin, and rolling it back up again. Then he pressed his fingers to the inside corners of his eyes.

I reached for his hand, and said, "Yes, of course, honey."

Perhaps it was my love for him that made me lie. If so, then my theory was correct—love disrupts peace.

———

In my second trimester, lying on my bed, I would often imagine cutting my wrists, my blood dripping onto the floor, the life of my fetus slowly ending before he was ever exposed to the hardships of life and a mother who did not love him. *What if the fetus absorbed not only my nutrition but also my feelings? What if my daydreaming imposed abandonment issues onto the child?* Instead of my blood, my tears stained my pillow. I turned to look at Levi and placed my hand on his ribs, feeling them expanding and contracting, and I imagined his reaction at finding me lifeless beside him. So, I kept the fetus alive. Not for the baby. Not for Levi. I kept it for myself.

———

Alex was born with the look of a famous Japanese boxer who later became a slapstick comedian. His face red and beaten, his body bruised. When I pressed him to my breast to feed, he could barely open his eyes, his eyelids still swollen, like an alien . . . no whites to his eyes.

"He's here! He's in my arms!" I shouted to my mother in Japan over the telephone. "He is as red as a baboon's butt and looks like Guts Ishimatsu. Mother, he is here with me, and when I hold my finger under his nose, I can feel the air coming out. He is alive!"

My mother laughed or cried or both, and said, "He sounds adorable!"

"Yes, though it doesn't make any sense."

"Why does it need to make sense?" my mother said.

———

Two or three times in winter, when my bed is too cold to put my feet in, I climb up to Alex's loft bed and nudge him awake.

"Alex, Lex, Alek, Lexy, Lulu. Lala. Come to my bed," I say, tickling him under his arm. He mumbles in his sleep and turns away from me. "Alex, come sleep with Mama," I repeat. He doesn't move and his body feels like a dense log. After several shakes and whispering into his ear, he gets up, his eyes still closed, and climbs down the ladder. I hold his back to save him from falling, and when he reaches the floor, I carry him to my bed. Our feet intertwine, his feeble hand lying on my cheek, and I am not cold anymore.

———

I have been collecting Chinese zodiac holiday cards. I've written fifteen of them so far and sealed each in a brown envelope. My brother is a good man who keeps secrets to himself. He is also a world traveler who spends every bit of vacation time outside of Japan. When Alex leaves for college, I'll give the envelope to my brother and tell him to send one card to Alex every year from some foreign country. I picture Alex saying, *My mother! She is the happiest woman I know. Last year, the card was postmarked in France and this year in Brazil*. And I'll smile under the cold rain with an image of his smile.

———

This morning, I leave Alex untouched and walk to the kitchen. I turn the oven on to broil, crack two eggs in a bowl, add some milk, whisk, and pour the mixture into the pan. I put a piece of frozen hash browns into the oven and toss two slices of bread into the toaster. I make breakfast for myself too, so Alex can have someone to eat with. Eating breakfast alone is what lonely kids do. My son is not lonely. I won't allow it. I know I don't deserve to eat but if I don't eat who is left to love him? I make two crosscuts on the top of an orange to peel the skin so that he will eat the fruit and not just suck the juice. I pour some milk into our cups. No coffee in my house. Alex is still too young for it and I don't buy this luxury item for myself. I take the hash browns out of the oven and place them on his plate and wonder where I went wrong.

The alarm goes off and it's time for him to wake up. His lips part slightly; I inhale his exhale. His seaweed breath. I can't resist consuming it.

"Baby, it's time to wake up," I say.

He wiggles, pulling me into my bed, and buries his face in my lap. I freeze.

"Five more minutes," he pleads.

"No, time is up."

He grumbles but rolls off the bed and walks to the bathroom. I see his back standing in front of the toilet then hear the trickling sound. "What's for breakfast?" he asks, washing his hands.

"Same as yesterday," I reply.

There is no one in this house, just him and me. There is no one he sees in this house, just me. And there is no one I see in this house, out the door, or anywhere, except him. Who is going to love him if not me?

We sit across from each other. The food is still warm, just perfect.

"Do you love me?" I ask him.

"Yes, why?"

"Because I'm happy," I say.

He shrugs.

It hurts to be happy.

"Ms. Smith told us about heaven and hell yesterday," he says. "She doesn't believe either exists because when she was a child the teacher at Sunday school told her her dog could not go to heaven with her, only humans can."

"That's funny," I say. "What do *you* believe in?"

"I believe in everything, heaven, hell, reincarnation, the field of punishment, and the field of Asphodel. How about you?"

"I don't believe any of it."

We finish our breakfast. He brushes his teeth, changes his clothes, and grabs his backpack. Just as he reaches for the doorknob, he turns around, and looks at me. He says, "Yes, you do, Mama. I know you believe something."

# Hire Me

MY DEAD HUSBAND VISITED ME IN MY DREAMS, AGAIN. THIS TIME, HE came to kiss me.

I kept my mouth closed. "I didn't realize you were coming to see me today," I said and shut my mouth again, tight. His tongue stretched and touched my lips and my mouth sealed itself even more tightly. He didn't force himself on me. He licked my lips, waiting for me to let him in. He had a mischievous smile. He looked innocent, not hurt by my behavior, and that disgusted me even more.

I endured my husband's licks until I woke up. He was still forty, the age he died. I was the age I was now, not quite forty, just getting there, but I felt older compared to him.

Men are merely a distraction to life. They approach you sweetly, inject a love potion inside you, then die, leaving their offspring and credit card debt. If I were a praying mantis, I could at least bite off his head and eat him to keep me alive until the child was old enough to survive alone. His death wouldn't be a waste. But I was a human; besides, how good could a male brain be anyway?

No one ever came close enough to stimulate my hatred in my waking life. No one ever came near enough for me to feel hatred. But in my dream, his tongue stimulated my hatred. How could I hate him now, when I didn't while he was alive? In the dream, I was safe to think like that without guilt.

The whole dream lasted probably one minute, but it felt longer. And just like in my waking life, the time flew away when I was having fun, but when I was struggling, the time didn't let me go. In the dream, the place is always defined, but when you try to define the place in your waking life, the place disappears. The dream could have occurred in my bedroom in my current house, where no one slept with me, or it could have been in the old house. It could have been anywhere and nowhere. Such clichés could exist in dreams without apology.

"I love you. I'll take care of you," he used to say when he was still alive. *Take care of you*, to hear that from a man always felt like a privilege to me. "You're so lucky that you get to be with our son all day long. I wish I could do that. But someone has to make money, right?" he said that too.

His words were kindness mixed with pride. But what I heard was that I was eating up his money and happiness.

*Are we going to lose our electricity tomorrow? How much are we really in debt?* My husband was struggling with his business. I had no idea how much money he actually had or did not have. "Oh, no, you shouldn't be worried about such things," he would say. "With my business and mortgages, it's too complicated for you to understand our finances. We'll survive. Just focus on raising my child." *I have to make more money. I have to make more money,* he said every day when he was changing his clothes, when we were eating breakfast, and when we were out on the weekend. "You're such a great mother. I'm so happy." He also said that in between his money talk. I knew he spoke honestly. But what I remembered was he couldn't be with his son because he had to feed me. How could I make a man who loves me so unhappy by having his child? He loved our baby. He loved being a father. Then, I thought, it must be me. My existence.

*Who would hire a nonnative English speaker without any job skills? Aha! I could babysit while I watch Alex,* I suggested. "No, it divides your attention. No, someone needs to be with him. Don't worry about money. I'll take care of you." So, my idea of supporting each other was rejected. He was stressed because of me, but he was happy that he had a family.

Our newborn son needed eight diapers a day. One box of diapers lasted fourteen days and one box of diapers had cost fifty dollars. I could stretch a box for two months if I let Alex go diaper free for an hour or two a day. What would the harm be if he peed on the carpet?

At the hospital after the delivery, I lied to the nurses that I was bleeding badly and needed more sanitary pads. They gave me ten pads a day. I limited myself to one a day. If I kept nursing, maybe my period wouldn't return for seven months or even two years? Twenty-seven pads would last three periods. The extra six dollars would buy two dozen eggs.

I calculated $350 a month as the minimum amount I needed for groceries and suggested Levi give me that amount. He said, "Nonsense, you can use my money all you want. Here, use this debit card."

When I tried to use the card the transaction was rejected. *We must be very poor,* I thought. *Or it could be that's how much he values me.* I told him, "Once a month, just put the amount you can afford in our joint account, and I'll manage." He said, "No, you can use all you want. Just let me know before you go shopping, so that I can make sure I have enough in the account." A piece of plastic (but with no money) was my lifeline. What would happen to our baby and me if he got in an accident or if I made him so mad that he decided not to feed me?

"Hire me as Alex's mother," I said. "You can pay me minimum wage for taking care of our child. I'll buy groceries and diapers from the money you pay me. Of course, I'd do all the other housework too." *Even sex,* I'd add that on top, I thought.

"Hire you? That's ridiculous! No, raising a child is priceless. My appreciation is beyond money," he said.

Perhaps I was experiencing postpartum depression, and therapy could help, Levi had suggested. I had been asking him to sign up for a life insurance policy for months. He told me, *tomorrow, they are expensive, and I have to find the best deal.* A therapist cost $80 per session. He would pay $320 a month to fix my sex drive, but he wouldn't pay $100 a month for the life insurance premium.

A night after my first therapy session, I gazed up at the ceiling, Levi on top of me and my legs wide open like a dead frog on the road, then a thought came to me. I would not be able to keep this ceiling over my head if he suddenly died. It hurt. The penetration hurt. *The life insurance could lubricate me.* When my malicious spirit took over ownership of my soul, I held my knees with my hands to keep my legs open to bear the burning sensation from the friction between foreign fleshes. My face tightened as I relived the pain of the vaginal tear from the birth of my son.

"Your body is refusing me." He stopped and went to the bathroom. Seeing his sad behind, I felt an evil sense of victory rising in me.

At the time, my husband's newest obsession was getting tattoos. "Tattoos are a form of art. It's time for us to embrace them," he said. One afternoon, he left his work at noon and when he came home past dinnertime, I saw his arm wrapped up with Saran Wrap. "Look, honey! Isn't it gorgeous?" The ten-commandment stone, the size of our son's head, was etched into his left arm. "How much did it cost?" I asked.

"Hon, you don't ask the price of art. I'm asking you if it looks good on my arm," he said, and I thought it could be beautiful, if it were a framed drawing that we could sell.

"Next time, I'm going to have them tattoo our son's face on my other arm. Unlike clothes, tattoos can stay with me forever," he said.

At the time, the newest piece of clothing I wore was the cardigan I'd bought from a discounted store. I didn't realize the left sleeve was sewn in upside down until I put it on. The seam was visible from the top of my shoulder along the full length of my arm. *Ha! I have no left sleeve, but we have a sleeve tattoo.*

And indeed, he did take the piece of art to his grave.

If he knocked on my door today, I would not let him in. "I don't want your protection. I don't want your love. I don't need your money. I want you to hear me and see that I'm capable." That's what I would say to him before I slammed the door on him.

# Failure

"TAKE THIS BOX TO THE RECYCLING BIN, AND ON THE WAY, GET THE trash by the stairs!" I told Alex, who had finished swiffering the floor and was now lying on his bed reading a comic book. One, two, I counted how many seconds it took him to get up . . . Twelve, and he was still not up.

"Alex, take that box and the trash by the stairs now! Otherwise, I will throw away your board game."

Without answering me, he stood up, carried the cardboard box, and ran to the stairs.

"Don't forget the plastic bag by the stairs," I screamed behind his back and heard him say, "Okay, Mama."

A few minutes later the washing machine buzzer went off, and I went downstairs. As I carried the wet clothes to the dryer, I spotted the plastic bag with dog paw prints on it under the stairs. I shoved all our damp clothes into the dryer, set it on delicate for sixty minutes, then screamed, "Aleeeeex!" I dashed upstairs with the plastic bag in my hand. We met in the sunroom.

"Why is this under the stairs? I told you to take it to the trash bin," I said, dangling the bag in front of him.

"I don't know," said Alex.

"How can you not know? Who else would move the trash from upstairs to downstairs?"

He shrugged his shoulders and looked at me indifferently.

"Alex, did you wash your hands when you came into the house? Yes, Mama. "I see blue paint on the back of your hand." "Alex, did you give your teacher the field trip slip?" Yes, mama. "I got a phone call from Ms. Smith. She is missing your field trip slip." "Alex, wash your hair"—yes, Mama—"and you come out with your hair dry. You are lying to me again, Alex. Are you always going to lie to me?"

He said, "No, no."

"Take this trash to the trash bin, please."

He took the bag and passed me.

"And what else do you hide under the stairs? Homework? Dog poop?" I said as I heard his footsteps becoming fainter and fainter.

I dropped onto the couch in the living room and stared at the photos of the three of us together in front of our old house, only a few houses down from where we lived now. Alex in Levi's arms, we were all smiling, even me. I wondered what Levi would say about his son lying if he could see us now. I wondered if I'd made a mistake moving back to San Francisco, taking Alex away from his Boston family.

I saw Alex coming through the kitchen and toward the living room, skipping and humming.

"I think I have failed as your mother," I said.

He stopped by the entrance to our living room, and began to climb the entranceway using his hands and feet like Spider-Man. He gave a big nod from the ceiling.

"What should I do?"

"I don't know."

"I don't know either. I raised you to become a liar."

He reached out toward the ceiling with one hand while the other hand still held the entrance molding. "Look, I am almost there!"

"I don't demand too much of you, do I?"

"You do." He nodded three times.

"Then I quit! I will quit being your mother. I'll feed you, take you to school, and tell you to go to bed. But that's all. Otherwise, we don't talk to each other."

He looked down at me from the ceiling.

"In thirty minutes, we are leaving for the grocery store, and I have to take you, because if I leave you home alone, I'll be deported."

Alex jumped down, skipped away to his room, peeked out, and said, "Can I buy something?"

I ignored him.

At the store I walked a little faster than usual. I did not hold Alex's hand and he did not ask me to either. Even in the parking lot, I didn't; instead, I motioned for him to stay right behind me. We walked like a mother and a baby duckling; except I was not his mother today.

Out of the corner of my eye I saw him trotting, trying to catch up with me. He almost crashed into a mother with a baby in her cart, ran between two teenagers, and dodged under the store clerk stacking some glasses on the shelf. I know my son. I could see his every movement without looking back. But I didn't wait for him. I was not his mother. I walked at whatever pace I chose.

I normally stop by the toy aisles because Alex likes to look at the boxes and make up stories in front of the displays. Usually, Alex's hands will fly in the air as if he was holding the tiny toy figures. "To the moon, no, to Mars! I am your father. No, you are not!" His world is a mixture of his favorite movies and cartoon shows. If I let him, he would go on playing for thirty minutes and more. He'd squat there with empty hands. His cheeks would be blushing as he'd occasionally spit to make the sound effect of an explosion. I'd stand behind him and listen, trying to find out if he'd felt the absence of his father, trying to listen for his suppressed emotions, sadness, a void, things he might keep to himself. I wanted to know where I went wrong and what he was missing. But his world never seemed to cross over into reality.

He didn't ask me to buy these toys. I realized that to him, it's enough to have them all in his hand, in his mind.

But that day, I passed by this aisle and headed to the cleaning supplies aisle. When I got there, I realized Alex was not behind me. I went back to where I came from and peeked into the Lego aisle. He was there, like always. I wanted to yell at him, "Alex!" but I was not supposed to speak to him. Standing behind the Barbie dolls, I continued to watch him. He didn't notice that he was away from his mother. I finally came out and stood next to him, lightly touching his shoulder. He looked up at me. I began to walk fast, and he tried to keep up.

I grabbed dish soap and when we arrived at the cashier, I also grabbed five gift cards.

"Mama? Can I buy gum with my own money?" he asked and showed me his wallet. I saw two big front teeth, too big for his small mouth, when he smiled at me. Suddenly, I wanted to smile back, but I was not allowed to. He placed the bubble gum onto the black conveyor belt next to my gift cards. I moved it to the edge, the metal part where it did not move to the cashier. He put it back on the belt, I removed it again. He put it back again, and I gave him a stern look, and he got it. He reached for it and held it in his hand.

The cashier scanned the dish soap, then asked me, slowly, carefully pronouncing each syllable, "HOW MUCH WOULD YOU LIKE TO PUT ON THE GIFT CARD?" While I was thinking of how much to put on it, I saw her writing numbers, *ten, twenty, and thirty?*

"Oh, no, no. I hear fine. My voice works fine and I speak English fine too. I just was trying to teach my son . . . Twenty each, please."

The cashier tilted her head, crumpling her note. She scanned the gift cards and put them all in a plastic bag.

"And what are you getting, mister?" she asked Alex. He bought the gum with his own money.

The food court was crowded but we managed to get seats. I didn't ask Alex to choose what he wanted. I pointed to a seat at a table. He sat and said, "Mama, I want a corn dog!"

As I waited in line for the food, I stretched my neck to see if Alex was still at the table. He was swinging his legs and gazing at a large Christmas tree. I raised my hand to wave, but before I made the waving motion, I stopped. I wondered if I was already failing in my attempt to quit being his mother.

Alex began to play with his package of gum. He pointed to something on the package, seeming to be pronouncing the words on it. He flipped it back and pressed his mouth on it. Then he decided to balance the package on the top of his lips. From that position he spread his arms in the air, like a propeller, and the package dropped on the floor. He picked it up, sat back in his seat, and stared at the gum, his eyes crossed. Without even trying to look at me to hide his sin, he unwrapped the package and ate a piece of gum. *We are having lunch!* I wanted to scream.

I came back to the table with two corn dogs, milk, and water. I sat in front of Alex. The scent of the watermelon gum was so strong that I could smell it across the table. It overpowered all the food.

"Good news, this gum is sugar-free!" he said, holding the package in front of me.

I saw his jaw moving up and down, and the fear of losing him rose up in me. "There are bad chemicals in sugar-free products. You have two choices: You can eat those chemicals and get cancer, or you can throw it away and live longer."

"What's cancer?" he asked.

"A disease that kills you. Do you want to die?" I asked.

His shoulders drooping, he walked to the garbage can and spat the gum from his mouth.

"I can't go a day without talking to you, Alex," I told him as he sat back down.

He nodded.

"We're all that we have. We must help each other. You understand? So, help me, Alex. What did I do wrong to make you lie?"

I saw the corners of his eyes begin to shine. His mouth shut tight, then opened. "Nothing."

"Nothing won't make you lie. See how you are lying now!"

"I only make you mad, Mama." He switched to English. "You always yell at me."

Tears filled his eyes. He quickly gripped his corn dog, bit it, and looked down. The noise of the crowd ceased as if they'd heard my boy's tiny voice. Alex bent his neck. I saw the whorl of hair on the top of his head. "I do, don't I."

My corn dog felt like a sponge in my mouth, so I stopped eating; instead I spent my time watching Alex eating his corn dog and washing it down with milk. He told me about the toys he saw at the store and which one he was getting from Bubbe for Hanukkah. *My boy, my boy, I am the one who is hurting, my love.* I nodded as he spoke, but inside I could only hear my own scream.

We walked back to the store, holding each other's hands. He hopped, which he always did when he was excited about something.

We returned to the cashier to find gum with real sugar. Alex and I read the nutrition facts on every package on the shelves. We went through them one by one, top to bottom, but didn't find any.

"I'm sorry Alex. It doesn't seem to exist," I said. "I was wrong. I was the one who was wrong." I crumpled to the ground and covered my face. I couldn't bear myself any longer. I wanted to take back all my yelling from his birth to now. How could I hurt the one person I cared about in my life?

"It's okay, Mama." He squatted next to me, patted my head, and said, "We're okay."

# Nukegara

WE GO THROUGH THE FOREST BY BICYCLE, AMONG THE CICADAS' FULL chorus.

"I'll bet we can find them easily in this place."

I speak to my son, who is riding behind me, on the child seat attachment of my bicycle.

"Yeah, but they are also brown."

He had met cicadas for the first time here, in Japan. We live in a town where the summer is too cool for them to grow and winter too warm for sleeping.

"Don't you worry. I used to be good at this," I said.

My childhood summers belonged to my mother's birth home in Kumamoto. I remember when my grandmother was still energetic. Besides chatting with her neighbors, she had no hobbies. As soon as she finished her breakfast, she left to visit her friends. When the noon siren echoed in the town, the front door opened, and before I knew it, my grandmother was in the kitchen preparing lunch for her husband and herself. They ate lunch together; only the sound of biting into pickled cucumbers kept them company. Each dish they emptied she immediately took to the sink, washed it, still chewing her food, then sat back down next to her husband. When all the dishes were clean, she said only, "I am going." Then she left again to chat until the five o'clock siren sounded.

My grandfather, who was blind, often walked along the wall the whole afternoon, calling my grandmother's name. In a haiku, he wrote:

*Fine autumn day*
*My bullet wife*
*nowhere to be seen*

My mother wrote this haiku down with a fude. It is still on the wall in front of my old desk, next to a faded Audrey Hepburn poster.

I heard about my grandfather's death long after he'd died. My mother telephoned one night and told me the news, speaking as if she was telling me about my cousin's wedding.

"When did he die?"

"Three months ago. I did not tell you because I thought you were too busy studying. I did not want you to feel guilty for not being able to come home."

I never witnessed my grandfather growing weak. In my memory he still walked along the wall, calling my grandmother's name—bright and healthy. I was glad that I kept his haiku.

My grandmother grew weaker, not because her husband died but because her dentures no longer fit, giving her pain when she ate. She moved in with my parents and lived her life as a sick old woman. She lived each day full of enthusiasm only to die. According to her doctor, though, she was perfectly healthy and she told my grandmother that she wished all her patients would take care of themselves as well as she did.

Before the sun was up, my son and I ventured into a forest to catch an elephant beetle. On the weekend we swam in a giant pool attached to the amusement park.

Every day was a new discovery for my son. However, this wasn't so for my grandmother. When we spoke to her, her gaze passed us as if there was something better waiting for her up ahead. The only change our visit brought to her life was that she now had to wait for the bathroom.

I don't recall her speaking, not even once during our visit. Her voice only existed in my memory. For what reason did she stay so healthy?

"Let's find a cicada." I parked my bicycle by the sidewalk.

"But I don't see them," Alex said.

"Mom can find them," I said.

Even though the cicadas were screaming, I could not even find one. They were invisible.

They have only one week to live: What kind of cicada would be suicidal enough to scream in the lowest part of a tree? If I do not find one my son might grow up to be a man who gives up easily. I looked for one for my pride and for my son's bright future.

"Look, it's a nukegara." I grabbed it and showed it to him.

"Is this a cicada?"

"No, this is the shell which the cicada stayed in before he became an adult, like the cocoon of a butterfly. It was a house for him to grow up in. Hold it."

He touched it with his index fingernail. The shell rolled in my palm.

"No, I don't want to."

"Why? Are you scared?"

"Yeah."

"It's okay. It's not going to move."

"I know."

"It's rarer to find this than it is to find live ones." This was a lie, of course, since every cicada has its nukegara.

"It's hollow. It's creepy."

I let it fall. The brown shell settled slowly and blended in with the ground.

The cicada chorus grew louder.

We continued our bicycle ride among the trees.

"Cicadas live underground for seven years like a baby in a tummy. Then they come out and live in the shell before they become a cicada and fly away, so it was not a dead cicada," I said.

"They never go back there again?"

"Never."

"Why?"

"Because they can't fit there anymore."

"Where is their home?"

"They don't have one."

"No home?"

"No home."

# The Free Range

MY BROTHER'S DEAD SKIN CRUMBLED IN MY MOTHER'S PALM WHEN she rubbed the purple ointment into his back. It's a special kind of ointment, my mother had told me, that keeps his skin moist and heals the scratches. It smells delicious, like roasted sesame seeds, I told her jokingly, and she responded it did contain sesame seed oil.

My brother lived with my parents just as many of his single friends did. He graduated from Japan's equivalent of an Ivy League college with honors, became a consultant at the hottest tech start-up in Tokyo, and just last year, won the Good Design Award, given to the best web engineer in Japan. Unlike his friends, he contributed to my parents, a thousand dollars a month, while also paying off his student loans. This man, my brother, was sitting naked, not even wearing a towel—crossing his legs in front of me, his nephew, and his mother.

"I can't believe you can get *atopic eczema,* even here," my mother said, gently pushing his penis to the side to rub the ointment into his testicles. My brother said nothing—mornings he was too sleepy to respond.

His penis was rough and dry with innumerable cracks and wrinkles, and the closest thing I could think of was an elephant's trunk, except it wasn't gray. His entire body was red because of the inflammation and because while he slept, he scratched his back like a dog on the ground till he bled. I imagined my brother as a red elephant with his trunk hanging between his legs, though his human head still sat on his neck. It didn't make sense, but again his disease did not make sense to anyone, not even his doctor.

"You are lucky," my mother said to my brother, "because as long as you wear long sleeves, no one will see your skin." She wiped my brother's dead skin bits off the tissue.

"No, because I am good at what I do, and that's all that matters," he said.

"With your shirt on, you look just like everyone else," my mother said.

I saw red dots on my brother's feet as if someone had etched a distorted version of an American map; eczema had finally reached there. My brother slapped his neck several times. He knew scratching could make his eczema worse, and even if he wanted to scratch himself, he couldn't. He cut his nails so short that we could touch the soft tissue between his nails and his fingers.

It was a hot, humid morning. The air conditioner had been running since five o'clock. My brother set the fan to full swing and as the fan began to rumble louder Alex turned the TV up.

"Hey, time for your breakfast. Turn off the TV," I told Alex.

He let out a sigh, sitting down at the table in slow motion. With the TV off, the noise from the fan became louder.

"What time are you picking me up?" Alex asked in his perfect Japanese.

"Same as yesterday, two-fifty," I answered.

"Oh, maaaan." Alex stabbed his sunny-side egg with his fork. The yolk ran out the side. "When is summer vacation going to be over?" he said.

"What are you talking about? We are going camping, white-water rafting, and more. Besides, you are very fortunate to experience two different schools in two different countries. No one has that kind of privilege," I said.

"Well, Dylan has, Mayo has, so does Kai."

"They are also Japanese. I'm talking about your other friends." I gave him a stern look, meaning "no more discussion."

We were visiting Japan to see my family. Unlike in America, Japanese public schools continue through July. *We welcome foreigners, diversity, globalization!* the principal had said when I asked if Alex could join their school to learn about his culture and to make new friends for the last four weeks before their summer vacation.

Alex had enjoyed school the past two years, but this year, he had been complaining about going to school as if he had just realized that he had been cheated on his summer vacation for years. He was right, though I was not entirely wrong. At least, that was what I told myself.

"Done," my mother said, patting my brother's neck.

My brother cracked his neck, then put on his clothes. He now looked like a young businessman just like everyone else.

"Time to go. Say bye-bye to your uncle and your grandma," I told Alex.

Alex gave a hug to my mother, then waved to my brother and kissed me on my cheek. I saw him off from the window until his morning group passed the first stoplight and merged with other kids. Even from my parents' fifth-floor condo, I could see Alex slouching.

"Alex is not enjoying school this year," I said to my mom.

My brother left for work, and my father had gone to work long before I was up. Finally, it was her turn to eat.

"It's school, no one likes school," my mother said and slurped her miso soup.

"I know." I sighed.

"You still speak to him in Japanese, and he speaks back to you in Japanese even in America. What more do you expect from him? He doesn't have to learn something new. He just needs to go so he will be with kids his own age. Besides, what are you going to do with him for two months, just the two of you? *You'll* go insane."

"I know. But—"

"Let him suffer. Let him complain. Let him figure things out. He is nine. He is fine. You, on the other hand, need a vacation. Get a haircut, a new outfit, and where are your eyebrows by the way? People think we are sisters and that's not a compliment. Worry about yourself."

"You're right." As I said it, I took five bottles of supplements from the shelf by the dining table and lined them up in front of me; the labels written in Chinese, which neither my mom nor I could read.

"Remember the pill?" She pointed out the green pill bottle with her chopsticks, "Four years ago, that magic pill cured him." She nodded several times as her eyes widened.

"Maybe this bottle has expired," I said, looking at the bottom of the bottle.

My mother placed her chopsticks on the table. She dumped her small pickle dish into the half-full miso soup bowl and stacked the rice bowl on top; the heap of untouched white rice sat like a snow fort. She didn't finish her meal once again.

"You know, with this disease, you have to hit bottom before you get better."

Every morning, my brother bathed in body-temperature water mixed with vitamin C powder. He said that when he was in the tub, he felt best. He often fell asleep there until one of us went to wake him up.

After his bath, he came straight to the living room, turned the fan on low, and sprayed the special water. The wind of the fan brought the smell of the special water—the smell of a swimming pool. Just when the water dried out, my mother would finish preparing his breakfast and come out from the kitchen with his purple ointment. This had been their ritual for the last two years.

"You are lucky," my mother said to my brother, "because you don't have to go to work so early."

"No, because I love what I do for a living," he murmured.

Alex was eating his breakfast quickly today. He had swimming classes in the first and second period, his favorite subject at school. Opening Alex's backpack to put in his swimming trunks and towel, I found his folder, which had been missing for two days. Inside there were several handouts from school: an exam that was graded zero, a blank essay only signed with his name in English as if to protest for his American heritage, and from between them a neatly folded piece of paper slipped out.

"Mom, his teacher has some concerns," I said to my mother.

"Aren't you glad she's not his real teacher?" Rubbing the ointment on my brother's back, my mother said, "The dry patch is gone. It's healed."

"I know. But look at my eyelids."

My mother went in front of him. "It's showing up," she said.

"I can't go to work in the purple face," he said, laughing faintly. My brother stood up to get the steroid cream from the fridge.

The muggy air interrupted my sleep that night. Alex and I slept in the Tatami Room next to the living room, and I heard my parents speaking, quietly, in suppressed voices.

"Why?" I heard my mother say.

"Because it's not going to kill him," my father said.

"But he is getting better," she said and hit the table; the dishes clattered. I covered Alex's ears with my arm. I tossed my body slowly toward the living room. It was past twelve o'clock. My father was having a late dinner.

"But your health," my father said.

"There is a cashier at the Rainbow Market who wears a flower-print flu mask," my mother said. "I still remember the day she started working. She was only eighteen, right out of high school. I remember the day clearly because she was so friendly and the same age as Daichi. I noticed the dry patch of skin around her eyes and how she blinked constantly. I also noticed the red inflammation on her hand when she gave me change. Now ten years have passed. Every day, before I enter the grocery store, I pray that she is gone, that she finally found someone who loves her despite her disease. But she is still there, just as friendly as she always has been, yet hiding her face under the flu mask."

"He will be fine. The company loves him, he's got the award, not to mention his phone doesn't stop ringing because the headhunters want him."

"Don't tell me that you've never seen these people who are just there to bring you a paper and a pencil—people who they can't fire but can't use either. If he makes one mistake his company can send him to the mail room. All day he'll be licking stamps until his tongue becomes glued to the back of his front teeth. Can you imagine, our boy, my sweet, smart boy, being in at ground level, in a cold, dark, moldy room, at the age of thirty-one, the best time in anybody's life. He'll have no wife, no child, no house, and no friends. All day licking the stamps only to come home to his elderly parents. What will he have if we take his job away from him? Can you picture him coming home with his head down every day? Because I can't and if I try to imagine it, I . . ."

"He is fine. We know that."

"Don't you dare to stop me. He is getting better. I see it in him every day."

"Then please, just take care of yourself. That's all I'm asking," my father said.

I was going to peek in Alex's last-period class from outside the classroom, but the teacher found me in the hallway.

"I wanted to see if he was causing trouble in class."

"Oh sure. No, he is not causing any problems. It's just that Alex doesn't seem to be enjoying school, which I can completely understand. I would be the same if I were in his position."

"I know he cannot do exactly the same things as other kids in math and science, but he loves swimming, lunch, art, and being with other kids."

"I don't mind having Alex, and my students love him, but I'm thinking what's best for Alex. Perhaps there is a better way to learn Japanese culture . . . you know, with you and your family."

Casting my eyes downward, I spotted her wedding band, plain silver with one tiny diamond embedded, and imagined her life outside of school. Her husband comes home, gives her a kiss, and asks how her day was. She tells him she has a kid from America whose mother just dumps him at school. Although she informs the mother that the kid doesn't like being there, the mother doesn't listen. So he says, "The parents nowadays don't know what's important for kids." She agrees. They agree that when they have children, they will always listen to their children. *They* . . . it would not be her fault if she screwed up her child. It would be *their* fault, her and her husband. She doesn't know that if I messed up, it would all be on me.

"How about I pick him up after lunch," I said, "skipping fifth period because Alex loves eating school lunch. It's his favorite period." My heart was pounding, and I felt the pressure building within me. Still, I managed to respond in a sweet, pathetic voice.

After a long pause, she opened her mouth. "If you insist, sure, no problem. Again, I don't mind having him. As I said, I'm just thinking of what will be best for Alex." She paused again, smiled, and said, "And I hope you do the same."

I didn't feel like going home right away so I stopped by a park. It was empty in the late morning, only a few elders feeding pigeons. I climbed to the top of a castle-shaped play structure. From there I saw my parents' condo, my former piano teacher's house, and the rice fields. This park was once an abandoned baseball field, and I used to come here with my brother to catch grasshoppers and praying mantises. When we became bored with filling our insect cages, we splashed mud at each other in the rice field. We did the same loop the next day, the ballpark, the rice field, then back to the ballpark. Once, we even rescued a stray cat with a broken leg. We were probably seven and four years old then. As I splinted its broken leg, the cat held on to my leg. Her nails went into my calf so deep that they didn't come out. Both I and the cat tried to get away from each other. I, hopping on one leg, crying, and the cat jumping on three legs. By the time the cat's nails finally came out, my face was covered in tears and snot, and I saw three bloody dots in a triangle on my calf. I dashed to the water fountain and squeezed the wounds under the running water. From a distance, I saw my brother pointing out the cat licking its nails. The cat ran away as if it never had a broken leg. Seeing the cat's behind, its tail standing up like a walking cane, we laughed together so hard.

We had everything we needed, the rice field, the stray cat, and the freedom to be mischievous. These book-smart children in San Francisco wouldn't understand how the cries of a stray cat could drive you to rescue it, and how the pain of rejection could turn into a comedy in one second. A parent would spot the cat and help before the children could. America is not the land of freedom, at least not for kids.

For the next two weeks, our lives remained calm. Alex missed school for three days to go camping with my father and his friends. Almost every day, Alex's classmates rang our doorbell after school and they played at the park. He once came home soaked, telling me that he'd had the best water balloon fight in his life. Things were going well. So, when I saw the blinking light on my parents' phone, I didn't think anything of it.

His teacher had left me a message saying that Alex threw his textbook at recess because he was frustrated with math and the textbook accidentally hit the girl next to him. *The girl did not get hurt and Alex apologized to her. I just wanted to let you know because he hadn't done this before,* his teacher said just before the ending beep.

"Maybe I was wrong to send Alex to school. Japanese school might have traumatized him," I said to my mother.

"Then we all were screwed," she said from the kitchen. "Japan is built by a traumatized nation."

"It's our summer vacation. It's supposed to be fun. What am I doing?" I said and put my forehead down on the table.

The rhythmical sound of my mother cutting onions seemed to go on forever before she finally spoke again. "Can you bring an extra chair from Daichi's room? The company is cutting his hours. He is coming home early."

Later that night, in the living room, I looked up how other parents spent time with their kids during summer vacation. According to my research, rich parents hired nannies and took them with their family to Europe so that they had the family vacation experience while still having date nights, and single parents whose own parents didn't live nearby worked extra hours during the school year to save up money for a summer camp so that they could hold on to their jobs. This was because in America, if you let your kids play outside without supervision, people would report you to CPS.

And for me, that meant deportation!

I closed my laptop. It was past one and I heard a noise in the hallway; someone was coming out of the bathroom.

The living room door opened; it was my brother.

"Hey, what's going on?" I said.

"I am filling up the tub."

"Is it that itchy?"

He nodded and said, "I'm still taking Alex to the amusement park on Sunday."

"If you don't feel well, don't worry, I'll take Alex."

He nodded again and sat down on the floor in front of the fan, where he always sat in the morning.

"I don't care about my looks," my brother said, "Or maybe I might if my eczema starts showing up on my face, not just my eyelids but also on my cheeks, my forehead, and my ears. I don't know, I don't think so. Not like Mom does. But if I'm itchy, I can't sleep, and if I can't sleep, I can't work. It's so fun to create something out of nothing with other people, you know. First, a request from the client, then ideas, an outline, a prototype, and finally we launch the website. Do you know what I mean?"

I nodded, though I had no idea about the joy of making something out of nothing. The closest thing I could think of was Alex, but no one requested us to create him. Levi and I wanted him.

"Do you know where Mom keeps sleeping pills?" he asked.

"All the medicine should be by the teapot," I said and walked to the kitchen.

My brother followed me, and we searched the pills quietly, in the dark, careful not to wake anyone.

"Do you know how to take this?" I asked.

"Yeah, I've taken it before."

"Are you going to take it, then take a bath?"

He nodded.

"You are not going to drown, are you?" I asked.

"I don't think so," he said.

"Keep the bathroom door open."

He laughed soundlessly and said, "You looking at the shower door doesn't really save me from drowning."

"I'll feel better if I see the light on,"

He shrugged then swallowed the pill. "Don't tell Mom about this."

I nodded.

He went into the bathroom, turned on the light, and left the bathroom door open. I stayed another hour or so, and when his shadow appeared behind the frosted shower door, I left to sleep with Alex.

In America, Alex's teacher had told me that Alex was a high-level reader, an expert at Mad Libs without the usual obscenities, and always enthusiastic and full of curiosity. According to his real teacher, he was a great kid with a bright future.

We'd never had a president of the United States who spoke

Japanese. Over fifty million people watched Japanese anime nowadays in the U.S., and how many of them spoke the language? Alex spoke Japanese with no accent and more than enough to scavenge food and ask for the bathroom. Perhaps he could find his own stray cat, alone, in *his* foreign country, or so what if he watched cartoons all day?

"Hey, Alex. Do you know you can only be nine years old once?"

"Yeah." Alex was still in his pajamas, lying on his stomach and laughing as he flipped through his comic book.

"Life can be unfair. Some people are born rich, and others are born with incurable diseases, but everyone has the same number of hours a day. In that sense we're all equal and it's up to us how to spend the time."

"That's not really true, Mama. You know the theory of relativity?" Alex switched into English. "Einstein discovered that time is relative—meaning, the speed at which time passes is relative to your 'frame of reference.'" Alex air-quoted the last few words. "Meaning, there is no absolute origin. It all depends on the position of the observer, their time and space. Or their mood."

"What? Theory of what?"

"Think of it this way." He switched back to Japanese for me. "The time passes quickly during the swimming period, but it drags during the math period."

"Wow, that's well said. Anyway, what I want to ask you is: Do you want to quit Japanese school?"

He looked at me as if I was offering him cotton candy for breakfast. "Sure," he said. Alex began to hum the *Star Wars* theme song. I lay next to him. I kissed his cheek, scratched his back.

Suddenly, all my responsibilities lifted from my shoulders and a new sense of freedom arose. Yes, there was no land of freedom, but I could let my spirit free from my own self-restrictions. I hummed the theme song with him as loud as I could.

"You should eat, Alex," my mother called from the kitchen.

"Nope, no need. We quit," I said.

"Yup, we quit," Alex said.

"What do you mean?"

"Theory of relativity," Alex said.

"I'm letting my spirit free," I said.

A knife in her hand, my mother came from the kitchen and screamed, "Kids change their mind all the time. You decide what you want for your kids. Don't listen to your child!"

Alex and I sat up, our backs perfectly straight.

He looked at my face, my mother's face, then my face again, and said, "Uh-oh."

"Alex! Put your clothes on. You are going to school," my mother said.

Alex changed his clothes, ate a piece of toast, gulped milk, brushed his teeth, and went out the door. It was the fastest he had moved in the morning all summer.

From the window, I saw two kids from his morning group approaching him. The three of them began sword fighting with their umbrellas and I could hear him laughing all the way up on the fifth floor. Shaking my head, I returned to the living room.

"I still don't know what I'm doing, Mom. I don't have anybody to consult. I'm always up against two different kinds of parental values. I'm all alone in this parenting thing."

"Is that what you are struggling with? That's it? No matter how many parents the child has, two or ten, each parent carries their own struggles. Our pain cannot be divided by the number of parents. Whether it's pain or joy, they are only mine and only yours. Do you understand what I'm saying? Besides, no one knows what they are doing. You think his teacher knows? You think your friends know? You think your father knows? You think *I* know? We don't. Alex is only nine, and that means you're only a nine-year-old parent. And trust me, when you have a second one, you start over. You are back to a zero-year-old parent. I'm telling you the truth because if I was the expert, why would Daichi—"

The door opened, and my brother came into the living room. He turned the fan on with his toe, sprayed himself, and sat on his cushion as usual. As usual . . . except his body emitted a strange glare. His back was no longer red but gray, and murky yellow discharge spread across it like a spider's web. Each time he wiped the back of his neck, the discharge oozed through the wounds, a lava of pus flowing out. My brother, who had been denied the right to scratch earnestly, kept wiggling as if ants were crawling all over inside. He was trying to escape from his body. I dug my fingernails into my arm to scratch myself for him, and while swollen red lines on my arm faintly ached, I glanced at my mother.

She was crying.

The fan kept rumbling and she retreated to the kitchen. And I kept staring at my brother's grotesque back.

"This is good. You're getting better," she said, standing beside me, with the can of ointment in her hand. She sounded calm, just like yesterday morning, the day before yesterday, and years ago, when we were little kids chasing grasshoppers.

She walked to her son and began her ritual.

"I'm moving," my brother murmured.

"Moving where?"

"My friend's condo in Shinjuku. He is moving to Silicon Valley for a while. He said I can stay at his place for free."

There was an order in their ritual, first his back, his waist, then his arms. Little by little my brother turned purple.

"For how long?"

"For a year, possibly longer."

"For a year . . . or more."

He stretched his legs, and my mother rubbed the ointment onto his penis, his testicles, and his thighs.

"Let's face it, Mom, this is as good as it gets," my brother said. His voice was crisp and direct. I knew, even from his behind, that he was looking straight at my mother. And so did my mother, because even if she wanted to avoid his eyes, she couldn't. She still had one more job left—to apply the cream on his eyelids.

# 界面 (*kaimen*): interface

# The World Where the Sun Sets Twice a Day

I WAS AT A BAR IN THE EVENING, ALONE WITH A WHISKEY ON THE rocks, a drink I have never tasted in my waking life. The lead singer sat next to me. He said he was a screenwriter who sang about world peace at the bar, but really, he was merely a man who was looking for someone to love. He had dirty red hair and a pudgy body that didn't intimidate a woman of average physique. His whisker wrinkles etched at the sides of his eyes showed the shadow of wisdom. His sweet scent of pain from his boyish smile pulled me back to my teenage years, when I still pronounced "love" without having a cynical chill rush down my backbone.

After the show, I drove the singer back to his house. "You live three blocks away from me," I said. "Isn't it something?" he said. The rest of our conversation, in which we alluded to our mutual interest and sexual attraction, was erased, so was my ten-year-old son, who I cannot live without.

We kissed to say goodbye. When the inside of his bottom lip touched my upper lip, it electrocuted me. In a dream, it's possible to recall a somatic reaction I have forgotten exists in my reality. *I am wanted by this man.* The power of infatuation and positive delusion; it was possible to believe in the dream.

There was a party going on at my house. "Honey, I met them in heaven." My dead husband had returned from the afterlife. He stood on the dining table, conducting his new buddies as if they were in an orchestra. His friends loved to drink, eat, and sing aloud. Five dead men put their shoulders together and danced on the table with a song while they showered their spit on me. The soles of their boots mushed food as the bottle of red wine rattled with the rhythm of their steps. The bloody liquid dripped onto my clean white carpet. His new friends looked like pirates rather than men with tragic pasts.

"Hon, it's been a while, I need to have sex." My husband pulled me to the side.

"My fridge is empty. I need to go grocery shopping." I pushed him away.

I rode a bicycle to the grocery store farthest from my house. Inside the house was America, but the outside was Japan. The sky was burning. Like the aftertaste of the kiss, I simply accepted that the sun sets twice a day in this world. I ran to a phone box next to the grocery store. I called the singer and told him, "My husband come back to life, but I don't want him anymore. I want you." For nearly ten years, I was out of love and now I had too much love to handle.

It took me a while to realize the sun was rising, not setting. I was back in the world where the sun only sets once a day. Both the singer and my husband evaporated, while the touch of the singer's lip remained on my lip. Before losing the sensation, I closed my eyes, but in my awake life, I wasn't oblivious enough to believe I was capable of loving someone again.

# Why Do We Need Men When We Have Each Other?

LAST SPRING, WHEN BUBBE VISITED US, SHE SAT ME DOWN AND SAID, "Kyoko, I met someone."

According to Bubbe, a month prior to her trip to visit us, this guy from Switzerland, an accomplished architect who lives in Florida, out of nowhere, friend-requested her on Facebook. The casual text exchange quickly led to him calling her every day at 8:00 A.M. and 7:30 P.M., plus several short phone calls in between, on top of very long daily romantic love texts, which now added up to over sixty.

"Just FYI"—she raised her index finger— "I have never initiated a conversation with him. He is the one who calls me, and texts me long love letters. I am just replying to him. *Uh-huh. Is that so?* Remember, Kyoko, never chase a man. We are better than that. Let them want you. Let them come. Let them do all the work for you."

In the picture, he was gorgeous, dressed impeccably, and posed like a model for *AARP* magazine, in front of a house that might appear in the movie *The Great Gatsby*. A four-thousand-dollar French bulldog named George sat beside him.

"Bubbe, he looks incredible. How did you pull it off?"

"Guess what his first name is: Alexander. Yes, same as Alex. *Bashert.* I guess we are just meant to be," she said.

There was one problem, though, she told me, when Bubbe's tech-savvy friend ran the image search, Alexander's name didn't come up as a match. The gorgeous Swiss architect *did* live in Florida but with a different name, Joe Williams. Alexander Evans lived in a typical suburban house outside Miami. However, everything Alexander Evans had told Bubbe matched Joe Williams's CV, which her friend found on the internet—the company, architectural awards, his son's name, and a few more pictures with George the French bulldog. Only the name and address he gave her didn't match.

It seemed like either Alexander with an average house outside of Miami was disguising himself as Joe the gorgeous Swiss architect or Joe the gorgeous Swiss architect was disguising himself as Alexander the average Joe.

"I just want to know which one I'm in love with," Bubbe said.

"It doesn't matter who you're in love with," I said. "The initial stage of love only lasts so long, so enjoy it while it's there."

"My friend says it's a scam. What do you think, Kyoko?"

"Who cares if he ends up not the guy who you thought he was. Most of the time that's how it is anyway. Go for it. What's there to lose at your age? If he begins to ask for money, stop talking. And never, ever give out your personal information or your family members'."

"And sex," she said and raised her index finger again. "If he asks for sex. I should immediately stop talking."

"The term 'get lucky' applies in your situation, Bubbe. What are you saving it for? Sex, go! Money, run!" I said.

We eventually decided that Joe the architect was using his friend Alexander's name and address to hide his true identity to avoid attracting women who might be after his money. Bubbe and I named his strategy the "soul mate screening." After all, he was a handsome, accomplished architect who lived in the *Great Gatsby* house with a four-thousand-dollar French bulldog. The stakes were high. He must be careful until he was sure Bubbe was the one for him.

From that moment, every conversation with Bubbe was about the architect. Alexander told her that and Alexander asked her this. His favorite color was her favorite color. Her favorite food was his favorite food. They were completely in sync as if they had known each other before even the Earth was formed.

During my son's karate lesson when Alexander—now Joe, although we still called him Alexander because she was not supposed to know his secret and she could not take a chance of accidentally letting his true identity slip out of her mouth on the phone—called her, she stepped out from the dojo.

Alex had no talent for fighting. His fighting stance resembled a scared cat, his spine curled up and his hip pushed back out. If there were legs on his butt cheeks, they would be running outside the fighting ring before his sensei rang the gong. He was a Lego kind of boy—sitting on the floor for hours to build a castle or *Star Wars* ships as he pretended to be his little figures. He only continued karate because Bubbe and I forced him. Bubbe said to me, "Please, this was the dojo Levi went to. Alex must carry on his legacy. This is how I can remember Levi. Please do it for me. I'll pay for the lessons. Please."

Yet, yet! Bubbe stood outside speaking on the phone during the entire practice. I looked out the window once. She had a big smile on her face. I could almost picture her twisting her hair by her ear as she spoke like a teenager from an eighties TV show. When love presents itself in front of you, everyone, even the memory of your dead son, goes out the window.

At the dinner table, her phone stayed next to the silverware, ready to be picked up at any moment.

Even Alex told her, "Bubbe, no phone at the dinner table, please."

She told Alex that she must keep it to hear news from her friends. At her age, there was always someone who went to the hospital or heaven.

"Alexander writes well. The letters he wrote to me are like a novel. Read this," Bubbe said.

We were sitting together again on my bed, which Bubbe used during her visit. Alex was sound asleep, and we were looking for a classic movie to watch.

"I hate love letters. They make me cringe and want to scratch under my teeth. My response will ruin your romance," I said.

"You went to school for it. Read it, just one letter, please. You'll enjoy it like a novel."

"Bubbe, I did not go to a writing school to read your love letters. In America, I heard that, in order to find a good job, you must be a good liar. I went to a writing school to make up better stories."

"Well then, his letters will inspire you to write a new story. It could be your bestseller and you wouldn't have to bother finding that 'good job' you're hoping to get."

Finally, she won this battle. I looked at her phone.

Before I could think, I burst out laughing.

"He writes like a high school boy who is in la-la land. And why is it all capital? I even know that's not grammatically correct. And there's just something odd about this letter like—"

She slapped my hand and snatched her phone away. "How dare you! He's from Switzerland. He doesn't write very good English. You have no sympathy for those people who came to this country without knowing any English."

I wanted to say, *You're telling me?* But I decided to let it go.

"Don't you love to be romantic, Kyoko?"

"No, romance is a concept men wanted to implant in us, to tie us to marriage so that they'll have a live-in nanny and sex worker for their lifetime. And, marriage is a scam. You are the one who taught me that we needed it to survive, to open a bank account and raise kids. But you know what, we can build a wonderful life without them. I'm hoping to be the living evidence."

"I don't understand how you lived with my son. I know he was romantic. He bought you dozens of roses for Valentine's Day, no?"

I shrugged. "Bubbe, I'm having amnesia. I can't recall that part of my life."

Falling in love is about wasting countless hours by daydreaming, fantasizing, hoping and wishing, doubting and infatuating, and letting your heart break. I still believe that's the beauty of being human. I knew it once existed in me. I just couldn't remember that part. I felt broken. I began to sob.

"It's okay, Kyoko. I know you miss Levi," Bubbe said, and I wanted to say that that wasn't it. I really, really, really, really, really didn't miss Levi. The greatest gift that he gave me was the opportunity to raise Alex alone. What I missed were my feelings that arose from falling in love, the passion, the infatuation, and the heartbreak. My consumed mind. My courage to be a fool. I missed me, not Levi.

Bubbe passed me her napkin and her rocky road ice cream carton.

"It's all yours. Have the rest."

I held the soft container. The ice cream had melted, and countless almond bits floated in the brown milky pool.

"Bubbe, I know you spit back all the almonds." I pushed the container back to her.

"No, I don't. I push them aside."

"What do you do when you accidentally put them in your mouth?"

"I spit in my napkin."

"You're lying. See this? No nuts." I shook the napkin that she gave to me. There were brown spots everywhere, but no nuts dropped on the bed.

"Kyoko, forget about becoming a good storyteller or a liar. You know what we should do? We should go on a cruise and do stand-up comedy on a stage. I'll do the talking and you just respond. We'll make so much money."

"Cruise. Let's put that on your honeymoon candidate list. Do you think Alexander or Joe will take me on your honeymoon with you?"

We began to mentally prepare for her wedding in Miami Beach. She woke her newly bar mitzvahed grandson up to ask him to be her flower boy, and Alex firmly declined even in his half-sleep state. She asked me to be a bridesmaid, and I told her I'd be honored but just pick a dress that I could wear at my job at the preschool after her wedding was over. She asked me what she should wear for the first night of her honeymoon. I told her to buy something cheap from the Salvation Army because it would be off within two minutes anyway.

Soon we forgot that we still didn't know his name or his face, but at this point it didn't seem to matter to me (and never mattered to Bubbe, of course) because Bubbe was so happy, and I wanted her to stay that way.

"Kyoko, once I marry Alexander, I'm going to buy you and Alex a house. You shouldn't be living with housemates at this stage of your life. I've already asked Alexander if it was okay and he said yes; he even offered to build one!"

"Thank you, Bubbe, but I just want you to be happy. Don't think about me or anybody else. It's time for you to find happiness."

I was moved by her generosity, which made me cry even more than when she passed me the chocolate-stained napkins. We hugged each other tight, and she promised she'd make sure to bring us to Miami every year and start a new tradition with her new family.

"I always wanted to have what you and Levi had. Now, I will. Finally."

*It's like I'm having amnesia.* I thought about repeating the word to her, but this was her happy moment. I didn't want to ruin it with my own drama, so I kept quiet.

She confessed she'd never imagined someone would love her again—just her—not as a mother, not as a friend, but as a woman. Despite my cynical view toward love and my amnesia, I understood exactly how she felt.

Our dream ended when the architect told her that he had won an architecture competition and was moving to Malaysia in a week.

He said in order to continue speaking to her, he needed a new phone. A brand-new iPhone in red that had just come out. He even sent her a picture of it to make sure Bubbe would buy the correct one and the address to ship it to in Malaysia.

Bubbe had a brilliant idea. She offered to give him her Samsung phone, which was three years old. Then she would ask Ben to buy her a new one. Alexander said Samsung wouldn't work in Malaysia. It had to be the brand-new red iPhone. The phone call from Alexander kept cutting off, and Bubbe kept calling him back, and he kept claiming his phone was dying and he needed a new phone from her.

"I'd be glad to buy him a new phone if I could. But I cannot. I'm part of Ben's mobile plan. Alexander doesn't know how American cellphone companies work. He keeps saying, 'Go to Apple and buy one. I don't need a phone plan. Just that phone!' Poor man, he is from Switzerland. He cannot understand our system."

"Bubbe. It's a scam. Stop talking to him," I said. I was sitting on her bed as usual, watching our favorite murder mystery series. I heard the familiar 1920s jazz, a cornet solo, from the computer screen.

Bubbe didn't believe me. She locked herself in the bathroom and spent two hours explaining why she couldn't buy him the phone. She gave him very simple directions, step by step, loud enough for me to memorize from the other side of the door. "First, go to *Best Buy*. Bring your ID and credit card. Second, ask for cellphone service. Third, tell them to start the service for you. That's it. I know it can be intimidating to explain in English. Give them my phone number. I can explain to them what you want."

I heard Bubbe several times saying, *Nope, that's not the direction I gave you, repeat my directions after me.*

Eventually, she came out.

"All good! He said he understood and told me to forget about buying the phone!"

My dear Bubbe, even the scammer gave up on her.

Next morning, she was on the phone with him again. He apologized to her and told her he could not live without her. That was why he wanted a phone. He was not what I thought, Bubbe told me.

That afternoon, I researched dating scams and found a number of scam cases that originated in Malaysia. I read several cases about women who still sent money even though they knew it was a scam, just to have someone to talk to. *I know he will never meet me like he said. I know I am wasting my money, but what is the alternative?* they wrote. *I have no one.*

Until this point, I'd focused on Bubbe's girlish love affair and her happiness, but the moment I read those four words, I felt like I was hearing words from my future self. These women were me in twenty years. Bubbe was me in my old age. When I cared for no one, every man who passed by and who was on TV looked like potatoes, and all love letters I read in books gave me the sensation of my toenails being pulled. But I knew. I knew that if the potato helped me to grab some tofu from the top shelf at a grocery store and said, *I love this tofu, especially in miso soup,* as he passed me the package, looking into my eyes for five seconds, I would be done. Aloneness wouldn't bother me until the potato grabbed the tofu for me, but once I found my potato tofu boy, I'd realize I have been living in the bottom of a well. Love is cruel. Love is addictive. Love is dark. Love is cold. Potatoes are great. They blend with other food and last a long time in the fridge. So does tofu. I've been so careful not to fall into this well filled with love potion. I could grow roses in the well. Red, yellow, and pink, yes, I'd decorate my life with color. No more black, gray, and white for the new Kyoko.

When Alex becomes an adult living independently or with his own family, there will be nothing to stop me from loving someone, except . . . death.

The potatoes, tofu, well . . . as my mind took over like a runaway boar, the urge to tell Bubbe the truth became definite. I was the only one who could pull her out of the bottom of the love potion well.

I told her about my research. I waited for her to argue with me like she always did, but she was quiet. So I spoke. "Bubbe. You are not lonely. You have your kids, grandkids, and me. I know you know that you are not lonely. But these women. You marched with babies in strollers for women's rights. You've survived two shitty marriages. You are Bubbe. People tell you you're the queen of all women. You're the only person who could rescue us. Please report this guy to the FBI for the sake of all women in the whole world."

That evening, she slept through dinner. When she came out of the bedroom to the kitchen late at night, I was writing a story, an adaptation of *Thelma & Louise,* except the two main characters were a Jewish mother and her widowed Japanese daughter-in-law. They ran away in a classic Ford Falcon after the Jewish mother chased her stingy, unfaithful husband, Joe Williams, around the house with giant hedge shears, and possibly snipped off a bit of his most crucial body part "by accident." *I'm half the man I used to be.* Her husband might or might not have said this in his police report. Bubbe the Nipper, they named her, and the police began the investigation. Later, these two women would hop on a ship in the nick of time when a handsome cop, Alexander Evans (who had a secret crush on Bubbe the Nipper, and in fact was planning to escape the country with her), arrived at the port. The two waved and threw kisses at him. They'd make money by doing stand-up comedy on the streets of various foreign countries. Nope, I wouldn't let them die in the end. I'd rather make all men extinct before I see these two women die.

Bubbe sat down next to me and said, "I'll do it."

"Bubbe . . ." I slowly raised my head from my notebook and pushed my story aside. For Bubbe, my *Thelma & Louise* could always wait.

"I'm going to report him. I did my research and I think I can be a lady detective like Miss Fisher. Did you know these women paid thousands of dollars and some even spent their entire retirement funds? That is not acceptable. Kyoko, I'm going to do anything to help women. We women must always stay together and help each other, because men suck!"

*My bubbe! My idea was her idea from the beginning.* I didn't care how she interpreted what I had said, took it, made it hers, because all I wanted was to protect my friend, my dear bubbe.

That night, we sat on her bed as usual and watched a 1956 film, *High Society*. Bubbe claimed all dresses that Grace Kelly wore in the movie, including the wedding gown, and I claimed her casual clothes, including the white swim cover-up. It was a little game we loved to play. *I have this and you have that. I don't like that so you can have that.* We fantasized about wearing all the clothes and drinking Veuve Clicquot out of coupe glasses. We often divided starring actors too, but since neither of us liked Frank Sinatra or Bing Crosby, neither of us wanted either of them. *Why do we need men when we have each other?* I wanted to say, but right now men were a touchy subject for her, so I kept myself quiet.

"I was so close to moving to Miami. He could buy you and Alex a house. Things I wanted to do for you, I could do with him," Bubbe said and rested her head on my shoulder.

"I don't need anything, Bubbe," I said.

Eventually, Bubbe fell asleep beside me. I stroked her soft hair like I would do to Alex. I stopped the movie and slipped away from the comforter, trying not to wake her up.

This spring, Bubbe came to see us again, this time with a dating app, a kind of Tinder for people over fifty-five.

"Men love me. I've already gotten ten requests, and I haven't even put up my picture or profile yet!"

"Bubbe, remember last year?" I said.

"Kyoko, just because I had one bad experience, it doesn't mean all men will be the same. I am not going to let the experience stop me from putting myself out there."

We swiped each man's profile on her bed.

"Is it just me?" Bubbe said. "They all look kind of like an overused schmatta—wrinkled, stained, and torn apart. I want a man who is mobile but not outdoorsy, and younger than me so I don't have to take care of him later, but not too young so he won't leave me for a younger woman. He must be brave enough to put up with a person who suffers with arthritis, but not too much testosterone so I don't have to entertain him every night. I want someone who likes to watch TV with me at night and brings me ice cream but never complains about how much ice cream I consume. He must be circumcised, Kyoko, I don't know about how Japanese people feel, but I'm Jewish, ah-ah, not me, I can't do it. And at this age, I refuse to go down on him. Been *there* and *done* that. If you know what I mean." She rolled her eyes. "In fact, he can visit my bed, and when the movie is over, he can leave. We sleep in different rooms."

"I know the person who fits the exact profile," I said.

"Who? Introduce me to him," said Bubbe.

"Me."

"See, I told you." She slapped my shoulder. "We should go on a cruise. We'll do stand-up comedy and make money. We'll meet new men in every country we visit. We'll be the next Miss Fisher."

"Aha! Bubbe! I just figured out what was strange about the scammer's love letter. The letter never mentioned anything specific about you. Your name was never used in the letter, he always called you 'sweetheart,' and the flower he used in his similes wasn't your favorite!"

"Kyoko, that was a year ago. Are you still thinking about . . . what's his name?"

We stayed up until four in the morning, each holding a half-gallon ice cream carton and making up a scenario of Bubbe meeting a wealthy, generous gentleman so that he could take care of all of us. We would be repeating the same conversation the next year and the year after, happily.

# Never Ever War

ON AUGUST 15, THE ANNIVERSARY OF THE END OF THE WAR, THE BASE-ball players with buzz cuts, the spectators, the umpires, the coaches, and everyone on the TV offered a silent prayer with a noon siren. Those of us viewing the high school baseball tournament weren't forced to observe the moment of silence, but seeing the crowd looking down, their eyes closed, we couldn't refuse to give a minute of our life to the people who had died in the war.

In the midst of summer vacation, the time when children stopped caring about the difference between yesterday and today, an ice pop in my hand, I spent my afternoon zapping through the TV channels until an anime show appeared. I must have been in the third grade. I was home alone.

On the screen, the pilot in the cockpit spoke a few English words. The scene switched and something dropped from the airplane. The parachute opened. The ground flashed. A shadow came over the city. For a moment, a stillness like the silent prayer during the baseball tournament hung in the air.

The child who was kicking a stone paused and looked up at the sky. Then his skin stripped to burgundy, his flesh burst in pieces and melted. A dog screamed, guardrails thawed, windows shattered, and the town sank. An old man with a cane and a mother carrying a baby on her back: Their hair burned, eyes fell out of their sockets, necks were wrenched off, and they crumbled into ashes. When the mushroom cloud materialized in full screen, I crawled on all fours to the TV cord.

I've never seen the anime again. But that few seconds of the scene are printed in my brain. I can recall them even now as if it really happened.

No, it *really* happened.

Like a hypnotic snap-finger cue, the images I'd seen in the newspaper and history textbooks rushed back to my mind whenever I thought of war. But right now, in front of me, no people stretched their hands out begging for water without realizing they'd already turned into charcoal. No human shadow was etched on the cement ground. No mothers were holding their dead babies while maggots ate their injured legs. It was hard to wrap my head around the fact that the United States of America had been at war for years. Instead, in front of me, my two-year-old baby, his face plump and glowing lustrously, handed a cookie to a dog. For each cookie the dog held in his mouth, my son and I high-fived. It was in the middle of February in Massachusetts, and we were cozy in the sunroom wearing only short sleeves. The virgin snow glittered outside, and beyond that, the calm ocean lay without a single wave in sight.

My brother-in-law was an army man who owned a company; I was not sure how you could be in the military and run a business at the same time, but I knew it was true because blizzards, hurricanes, floods, mass shootings, whenever there was a national disaster, he was there.

According to my bubbe, Ben ran a consulting firm for big companies, both in the country and out of the country. What he was consulting about, I didn't know. If he was a website consultant like my brother,

I could picture his job. Maybe it was so complicated and so confidential that even Bubbe couldn't understand. His employees bustled in and out of his office to get his signature. Clients with concerned looks were ushered into the conference room, but when they came out, they all looked relieved, enveloping my brother-in-law's hand with both of theirs, thanking him for saving them. Some teared up. Others even bowed down although they were not Japanese. In just an hour, this man in a tailored suit could pull people out of their crises. But then I thought, did it mean he could bring people down to their misery in an hour too?

His rescue mission extended to his community. Twice, Ben had saved a high school boy from a frozen lake. The news quickly spread throughout the town and appeared on the front page of the local newspaper. In a peaceful town where the police's only job was to find a missing dog, the story of a local hero could for sure excite everyone, but my brother-in-law refused to provide his photo. LOCAL FATHER RESCUES HIGH SCHOOL BOY FROM FROZEN LAKE. "Father," although he had more impressive titles to distinguish himself from other fathers; it was Ben who chose the title, Bubbe had told me.

I witnessed one of his heroic moments myself. Once my brother-in-law stopped by San Francisco on his way home from a business trip. Levi and I picked him up at the hotel to have dinner together. At a red light on Van Ness Avenue, my brother-in-law rolled down the window and held out four twenty-dollar bills. Immediately, a man with a cardboard sign saying, "Cash Only" walked across to Levi's Ford Falcon and grabbed the bills.

"Bro, what are you doing? The guy might be an addict. Or this could be his day job and he's going home to his penthouse in his BMW," Levi said.

"It doesn't matter. He asked for help so I must help. That's the Jewish law," Ben told Levi in a matter-of-fact way, very quietly, his face as inscrutable as usual.

"Oh well. That's my brother. Major Ben can't help helping others," Levi said, patting his brother's head like he was his little child, and returned to belting out a song along with the radio.

Levi was a laid-back kind of Jew. He said his brother, on the other hand, belonged to a group called "Classical Jews," who observed stricter rules, but not too strict, like those who wore a yarmulke all day long. Ben's devotion to Judaism led him to sit on the board of his town temple. Wait, did Levi say Ben was a Conservative Jew? No, Traditional? I don't remember the exact name of the denomination, but basically, Levi belonged to the group where tattoos were allowed, pork katsu was permitted, and women who were not Jewish and not willing to become Jewish were still welcomed. There, our son could be Jewish and I could be whatever I wanted.

My Jewish brother-in-law, who saved companies from crises, rescued people from disasters, dove into a deadly icy lake for a stranger's son, and offered money to a guy who held a Cash Only sign, was going to a war.

Coming from a country that only had the Self-Defense Forces, I didn't know if you had a right to refuse to go a war or if it was all voluntary. My brother-in-law majored in war strategy; I heard his general say when Ben's wife, Anna, invited him over for dinner. Ben graduated at the top of his class, he'd said that too. Did it mean Ben was going to a war, to come up with a strategy to win? And to win a war meant . . . Maybe, in this modern world, there were wars that didn't hurt people. Or maybe there was a good war. A necessary war. But if so, that would allow lives to be destroyed for good. And who chose who was good and who was not?

"That's silly, Kyoko. Ben is like a teddy bear made from marshmallow," Bubbe had said when I confessed my fear about her son. "They are both born from me and raised by me. Ben is quiet and Levi never shut up. That's the only difference. In fact! In Jewish law, when the wife loses her husband, she marries her brother-in-law. Too bad, Ben is already married but he can take care of you and Alex. Just like Levi would have done, Ben will do anything for his family."

To me, Ben looked like the cold bronze statue in a history book rather than a sweet marshmallow teddy bear, especially when he stood in the grand foyer of his home in his long black wool coat and leather gloves. He had a square jaw, square shoulders, and a boxy physique. Like a wall between countries, nothing would pass through him, or pass through alive. The expressionless statue, of course, was quiet, and so was Ben. He rarely spoke at home and when he did his voice was utterly low, as if he was speaking to a pen in his chest pocket that I imagined to be a hidden recording device from his army.

If I had a way to measure our sadness, I know my sorrow would be nowhere near Ben's. My tears were a symbol of shame, and his silence was a symbol of loneliness. The premonition of hope. The healing that I could not touch, but I could feel the shapeless pale light growing in my heart. Somewhere inside I was confident that one day I would bounce back. I could have a new husband, but my brother-in-law could not have a new brother. I concealed this possibility within myself. To endure this reality, Ben must have been hoping to take responsibility for the person his brother loved the most. The only person who inherited his brother's blood. If Ben found evidence to put my love on trial, he would fight, using every power he had, to take Alex away from me. As Bubbe said, Ben would do anything to protect *his* family.

For a long time, I had dreamed of living in the States. I wanted to release myself from all Japanese shoulds and musts. *America is better. America is great.* I don't know who taught me that. Perhaps this was another paradigm shift after Japan lost the war. The possibility of being able to eat, to live safely, to become someone besides yourself, the immigrant's desire varies. What we have in common is that we were all lured by "possibility," enough to abandon our homes.

After I graduated from four years of college, I stayed in the U.S. to pursue a master's program in psychology, hoping a graduate degree would lead to more job opportunities. But the money I had saved in Japan was drying up, and I couldn't ask my parents to apply for more student loans from my father's work. I was this close to dropping out. *I wish some miracle would happen,* I used to confide to my mother. Twice, men asked to marry me. Both times my desire for freedom sobered me up and I said no.

*If I get married, I could live in America for the rest of my life.* A moment of reassurance resurfaced, as it had with other men, when Levi asked me to marry him. *Do I love him?* I kept asking myself. But the more I asked the more the line between love and safety blurred. An immigrant's love must be filtered repeatedly to the greatest purity. Even after you bring in a verdict of love, you must keep reexamining it and must keep proving to yourself that you married for love. The dusty framed picture of our wedding, children's graduations, grandchildrens' portraits hanging in the hallway; the most mundane miracle of life should be in the house before we finally let ourselves relax. And even if it was *the* love, it could collapse at any time.

That was why I brought up abortion to Levi at that diner.

*What is love?* Now, with Levi gone, I would forever be asking this question. But Ben might already know the answer. His reticence was a way to see through the lies of enemies. I wouldn't be surprised if such a mind-reading tactic was taught in the military of the world's most powerful country. I was the one who begged Bubbe to live with me in his house. But I was afraid of the presence of the head of this household. I sat in the furthest seat from him at the dinner table at the angle where he could not see me directly. I pretended to be asleep until I heard his departure door chime in the morning. On the rare occasions when he came home before anyone else, I prayed to Levi, who was his best friend, that I wouldn't end up eating dinner alone with his brother.

Luckily, I never needed to talk to him. There was always Bubbe or Anna who spoke for me. As long as I was careful not to be face-to-face with Ben, he wouldn't find out what I had with Levi. So, when the bell chimed and Ben entered the front door in his long black wool coat and black gloves, I wasn't prepared to hide from him.

I was supposed to spend the next few days with Alex and their elderly Great Pyrenees named Polar watching over this huge house. Laura's and Paula's families had flown in from Chicago and were already at their cabin. Anna and Bubbe had left with the girls this morning.

Alex threw Lego bricks and ran to the front door. He buried his body between Ben's legs.

Ben squatted down and held his hands out. Alex's small knuckles landed on Ben's open palms. Ichi, ni, san, shi, Alex said with each punch. "Good job, my karate kid," said Ben. "Keep your friends close; keep your enemies closer. Their long arms and legs won't be an advantage if you stay close to the enemy. You can take them down no matter how small you are."

"Hi, Ben? I thought you were driving to Vermont from work," I said.

"Anna forgot the sled in the garage," he said as he lifted Alex up. "And you? Didn't you go to Vermont with Anna and the kids?"

"No, I decided not to."

"My family can be suffocating. They always look so happy, don't they?" He smirked. "But you shouldn't be home alone. Why don't you come to Vermont with me?"

"No, it's okay. This is good for me."

"I understand that, but the cabin is big enough for you to get lost. That's what I do all the time. No one will find you."

"But I promised I'd take care of Polar. Laura is allergic to dogs."

"Hmm, then why don't I stay with you guys at home?"

"Oh no, no, Ben. I am fine. I am completely fine. I'm as happiest as I can be in here, alone. Go do ski with your family, please. You had hard few months."

"So did you."

"Make snowman," Alex shouted.

"A snowman?" Ben said.

"It's nothing, Ben. Anna promised a snowman to Alex before they left. But that can wait. You go ski and we make snowman when she return."

"But he wants it now."

"Don't worry, he is only two. He will forget it."

"My nephew is asking for help. He deserves a snowman. Actually, we can do better than a snowman. We are making an igloo."

Operation Igloo began. Alex looked like an astronaut ready to land on Planet Snow. Since Anna had already taken Ben's ski gear, Ben wore his army jacket and pants. Ben and I were worried about Alex being buried in the snow, so we put him in a baby backpack, and Ben carried it on his back. I didn't own any snowsuits, so I layered a bunch of clothes and topped them with a down jacket that Ben had bought me a few months ago as part of a welcome gift.

"Alex and I can handle this. Stay inside," Ben said and held his hand out to me and Polar. Two men walked out to the white-blanketed backyard.

Holding the top of the shovel that was stuck in the snow, Ben stood firm with his feet set apart looking as if he was assessing where to build the military base.

He dug one big pile of snow from the center of the yard and then another. About ten minutes in, Alex began to flap his legs and arms. Even through the window, I could imagine Alex screaming his favorite word, *Out, out, out!* Ben put Alex on the ground where he'd already shoveled the snow. Ben dug another pile, and just when he was about to dump the snow Alex dove into the little snow mountain. Alex was making a reverse snow angel. Just as I opened the glass patio door to go help, Ben shouted, "Kyoko, grab the sled from the garage! This shovel could split open Alex's skull. It's too dangerous!"

"Yes!" And I went back inside and ran to the garage. As I turned on the garage light, I realized I had never heard Ben shout before.

When I returned from the garage, Ben had already removed Alex from the snow pile, and they were back to playing. Ben walked to the edge of the yard holding the sled on his left. From there, he stuck the sled onto the ground and charged to the center with blistering speed. A big mountain of snow formed. Then again, he walked, and Alex followed Ben on the path where Ben had just scraped the snow. Together they pushed the sled to the center. Well, mostly Ben pushing and Alex chasing Ben's behind.

The mountain became bigger and bigger. I saw the green grass appear in a circle around the snow mound. My brother-in-law made a mystery circle in his backyard. Soon all the snow in the backyard would be gathered in the center.

I watched them from the door, jumping up and down to keep myself warm. Ben noticed me cheering for them. He came and put his jacket on me and zipped it up. The army jacket was much thinner than I'd imagined. *How would they keep them warm?* I thought.

"Trust me, we have the best technology in the world. This will keep you warm," he said as if he read my mind. He patted my shoulder and ran back to Operation Igloo. I checked myself in the reflection of the window. I looked like an army snowman. As I stood there conflicted between my outside appearance and inside belief, my knitted glove caught on the edge of his name tag. His last name, Levi's last name, Alex's last name, and mine. And I wondered if Anna had intentionally forgotten the sled in the garage.

The Japanese food that we ordered for dinner was horrible. Rice dry, avocado crunchy, and tempura soggy, but we polished it off, except Alex, who sat in the high chair between us. He turned sweet potato into Play-Doh and threw rice confetti at Polar. He was too honest to pretend anything.

Ben had a habit of doing something else while he ate. He had to multitask with his precious time. He flipped through the pile of mail. As he put aside the important mail to his right and the junk on the floor, he sighed and sipped a cup of tea.

"Everyone wants a piece of me," he said. "Hard work and determination can get you anywhere you want. Don't people know that?" He reached out for the Tums bottle, popped the lid open with his thumb, and shook out two tablets. "These people don't *need* my help. They just *want* it. It's a greed."

He growled and threw the Tums in his mouth.

"Was I your friend or enemy?" I asked.

He stopped flipping through the mail and looked at me. I could spot the slight surprise in his eyes. As soon as the words spilled out of my mouth, I wanted to run away, but his gaze was so strong that I was paralyzed.

"Ah, Sun Tzu. You are neither. You are my family who needs help. Also in English, we use present tense in this situation, because we are still family."

He smiled at me and returned to his task, tossing and keeping.

"Ben, I'm leaving here. I'm going back to San Francisco. I found a nanny job and house to share with a couple. I'm sorry. I'm taking my son away from you," I said.

He let out a single laugh through his nose, "Taking *your* son away from *me*?"

"I lost your brother. I lost your best friend. And now I am taking away the person he loved the most from you."

"I see," he said. This time, his eyes were still on the mail. "We call it survivor's guilt. It's very common among people who lost someone in an accident. You didn't kill him, and we don't expect you to live here forever. You don't need my permission to leave."

He put his hand on an envelope and ripped the top open. "Oh finally, I've been waiting for this one. This is for you. Good that it came before you're leaving."

I unfolded the letter and found a golden credit card with his name on it.

"Use that for anything you need, food, water bill, not just for my nephew but for yourself. As long as I live, it will work, even if you move back to San Francisco."

Another plastic card and another possible loss.

"Ben, do you have to go? To Iraq? You are the only son Bubbe has now. And Anna and the girls . . . I still don't know how things work in this country, but I know war is wrong. Everyone knows that, even children."

"There is a young man in my unit who has the same name as my brother," Ben said. "I've known him since he joined the army. He has a wife and son. I can't just send him alone and sit at home, can I?"

"That's a lie. Sounds too convenient. You made it up."

"Yes and no. Yes, I made it up, and no, because I know how painful it is for you to say that you lost"—he took a deep breath through his nose—"that you lost my best friend. I don't think I could live the rest of my life with that kind of . . . what is it called? I guess, that feeling of knowing I can save him if I'm there. I'm not going to leave him alone and let that happen again. I could save him, you know, I could save anything and anyone, if I was just there."

We moved to the living room. We sat as far as we could from each other on the long couch. Alex crawled up with us, going back and forth between Ben and me. While Ben was busy with Alex, I slid his gold credit card between the cushions. Eventually Alex settled on Ben's lap, but he only lasted there for a few minutes. He stood up and began tapping Ben's cheek, pointing at the TV screen.

"Wan wan, oyatsu ageruno," Alex said.

Polar stood up and walked beside Ben.

"You understand their language!" Ben said. "Your daddy and I, we spent hours trying to figure it out. But you got it immediately. My genius nephew. You're going to be a great man. You're going to make us proud."

It appeared to me Ben was talking about the people in the space-ship on the TV.

What Alex said was *Get me the doggie cookie* in Japanese. Because he had said it so many times since we moved to this house, Polar now must have understood the word "oyatsu." Alex kept pointing to the cookie jar by the TV stand, Polar's eyes on Alex and Ben, and my brother-in-law kept telling Alex a story of him and his brother. *Your daddy and I, your daddy and I.*

*Alex, hold on there, do not scream yet.* I was desperately sending him this telepathic message so that Ben could have a few more seconds with his brother.

My brother-in-law, who built the world's strongest igloo for his nephew, ate the awful Japanese food out of respect for his sister-in-law, and spilled out his survivor's guilt, was going to war.

Since we were children, we said never ever war. Losing the war meant losing the war, winning the war still meant losing the war. Nerds, athletes, introverts, bullies; this was one message all my class-mates in elementary school could agree on. *NO WAR.*

Despite everything I was taught, for this once, I told myself that Ben sincerely believed he could save all lives, both enemies and allies. And that was his war strategy.

# Ajumma

IT WAS ELEVEN O'CLOCK AT NIGHT WHEN I HEARD MI CHA'S FEET HIT-ting each stair through my ceiling. I came out of my room and we met in the kitchen. I sat across from Mi Cha and watched her crumbling her marijuana between her thumbs and fingers. On the tomato sauce jar where she kept her *supply*, the label said, "Life Foods! Made in Maui," and it had a small Hawaiian flag next to the writing. I smiled because years ago, while I was still a student and single, I had a va-cation boyfriend in Maui who grew weed in his backyard. With the money he made, he came to Japan with me. I never smoked with him, or with Mi Cha.

"What's the punishment for smoking pot in Korea?" I asked Mi Cha.

"I go jail," she answered.

"That's all? No death penalty? I thought Koreans are stricter than that."

"Come on, it's the country where people fix their faces like annual health checkup. We can't be that strict about changing our mood."

In this city, I couldn't afford to rent a place all to myself. For the first few years, Alex and I lived with a couple who had a dog, a Lab mix, and for another few years with a couple who had a springer spaniel. The first couple bought a house on the edge of the city and made a real family. And the second couple moved to Paris to start their careers. Mi

Cha's family moved into our house after the second couple moved out. Our plan: Mi Cha's family and my son and I were to live together for six months while they renovated their house to sell, a perfect length of time before we would become sick of each other.

As a mother who had failed to give her child a family, I could at least give him opportunities to make friends so that one day when he didn't want to talk to me, he would still have people to call his family. Whether as a response to my wish or his survival instinct kicking in, my son grew to be a social genius. It didn't matter where the kids were from or what kind of personalities they had; Alex had a way of striking up a conversation like he'd known them before they were even born. He attracted both shy types and outgoing types. To make good use of his talent, I was sure this country was the best place for him.

The first San Franciscan boy who memorized my son's name was Mi Cha's oldest son, Walter. My son's name came in a set of three for Walter as if once wasn't enough to reach him. What could be more popular than T-Lex for a two-year-old? "Lex, Lex, Lex." Walter loved to drop the "A." Even when Walter was too tired to walk, he'd lie in the sandbox chanting "Lex," and with what seemed like the last breath he had in him, he would reach his hand to my son, who would be making a sandcastle next to him. Mi Cha and I laughed at them, that Walter could never feel close enough to Alex even if their bodies fused.

My aptitude for socialization was the complete opposite of my son's. I didn't need a friend for myself, but with Mi Cha, I felt at ease. While our kids played at the playground, we talked about our home countries. Mine Japan and hers South Korea. We often made fun of each other's cultures. Once, Mi Cha taught me a Korean word, "ajumma," a word that originally signified marriage-age women, but as time glided on, came to be used to discriminate against a *certain* type of middle-aged woman. These women wore oversized, mismatched T-shirts and baggy pants, permed their short hair, and had outdated makeup or, worse, none. They chewed with their mouths open, spat on the ground, and pushed and shoved people out of their way to secure a seat on the train—they were women who had abandoned womanhood and had lost their grace. I told her we didn't have that kind of word in Japanese.

"It's a metamorphosis! It's something to celebrate! They don't take any crap from anyone. Even serial killers fear them," Mi Cha said. I want to be one of them, I told her and she said not yet, I'm not married and have not even reached forty. I stuck out my lower lip and sighed. And she added in a soothing voice, "Your life has just begun. You have no idea what's waiting for you."

The condo Mi Cha and her husband, Trav, owned had tripled its value in five years, but Mi Cha's mental health had only declined. At their house, they weren't allowed to walk, only to tiptoe. A hundred-year-old building in San Francisco, it had walls so thin you could hear someone burping next door. The downstairs guy who worked from home didn't know that in the morning Mi Cha and Trav each carried their sleeping boys to the bathroom, then to the kitchen. The loudest noise you could hear from their house in the morning was the boys drawing in their chairs and Mi Cha shushing them to stop. All the silence they created, the guy didn't pay attention, and every tiny noise he caught from Mi Cha's house, he complained. *Your kids are too noisy! Keep them quiet!*

Even when she lost her sister, Mi Cha couldn't cry without a cushion over her face. One night after she returned from Korea, I went to see her and found Mi Cha in the kitchen sitting on a chair holding her knees. I hugged her and she almost permitted herself to cry, but then she pulled away from me and put the tearstained cushion back to her face.

After her sister's death, she cut all her ties with the playground moms and asked me not to mention her sister again.

The downstairs guy also didn't know Mi Cha woke up one night, gave the boys and Trav a kiss, then went into the garage to search for a rope because she heard her sister's voice telling her to be free from her life. She felt a peace blooming inside her and had faith that her boys would be okay without her. Luckily, Mi Cha couldn't find a rope that night. She somehow walked back to bed and fell asleep.

"It's like we were meant to live together." Mi Cha pulled me back into our kitchen. "Three boys running around and babysitting each other, I cook, and you clean. Maybe I was Japanese in my past life, or you were Korean and we . . ." Then she licked the edge of the paper to seal the rolled joint. I could finish her sentence, but I didn't. I always waited until she implied permission. "Anyway, I don't care if we go bankrupt. I don't care if we can't find another house. This is where I want to be."

"You are not going to bankrupt. You are going to sell your two-million-dollar condo, then buy a single-family home."

"Can we just live here with you guys forever?" She tilted her head and spoke in a wheedling voice.

"Sure, but three active boys . . . Trav will have a nervous break-down. He must want a house of his own."

"He is okay with whatever makes me happy."

"He's a good guy."

"Yes, he is. My in-laws won't approve of this kind of lifestyle though. They are hoping that we'll move back."

"To where?"

"Exactly! Trav moved to this city to be away from them. San Francisco is made of these family refugees, don't you think? Look at me, I even crossed the ocean."

We laughed together and I so wanted to say to her, *Don't move, stay with me, be my family.*

"Come out to the backyard and keep me company," Mi Cha said.

We sat on the outside chairs. My backyard used to look like an opossum graveyard. Until one night Mi Cha pulled out a jungle of weeds and painted the wall aquamarine by the light leaking from our sunroom. The next day, she bought and planted broccoli, Swiss chard, mint, bok choy, and a lemon tree and called them "my *babies.*"

"I have to tell you funny story, Mi Cha," I said. "I clearly remember the last serious conversation I had with Levi. It was a week before Alex and I were leaving for Japan for the first time after Alex was born. I was watching Levi washing his old Falcon in the driveway. He said, *Enough of this guilt trip! Yesterday, Anna*—that was his brother's wife—*called me and said that I should come to visit Boston for the Jewish New Year because my brother might leave for Iraq to lead men to guard Saddam Hussein's prison and we never know what will happen. Then she added that after you guys leave for Japan, I'll be alone doing nothing anyway. Then today, my mother called me and said the exact same thing. If Ben wants to see me, he'll call. He's my brother. He's my man. Why can't they just say that they are the ones who want to see me? Why do they have to use my brother, Iraq, and guilt?* So I told Levi to say no and he did. He was so proud of himself."

"Good for him," she said, smelling the joint.

"Two weeks later, on Jewish New Year's Day, Levi died under the Impala."

"That's right." Mi Cha's eyes widened.

"When we landed at SFO, I saw my mother-in-law at the welcome gate. And she said, *I told him to come to Boston for Rosh Hashanah, but he didn't listen to me. I knew something bad was going to happen. Why didn't he listen to his mother?*"

"Have you ever told your story to your mother-in-law?"

"No. I just think I knew the reason. I had the answer to her question. I was the one . . ."

We lived three houses away from busy Army Street. Although ambulances constantly passed by, our neighbor's wind chimes and the rustling leaves in the big empty lot behind our backyard isolated us from the street noise.

"Right before my sister died," Mi Cha said, "she called me. I saw missed calls from her but I was putting my boys in bed, so I didn't call her back. The next day my parents phoned me and said that she was found dead." She clicked her lighter and took a couple of puffs. Then she slowly exhaled the smoke like blowing out a candle.

Mi Cha inhaled again, her head leaning against the chair back, her eyes slowly closing, and her mouth shut tight until she couldn't hold her breath anymore.

"What I want to say is that, Kyoko, if I die tomorrow, you must let everyone know that Mi Cha knew what happiness was and she had it here, in your house."

# The U.S. Government Wants Me to Live

THE U.S. GOVERNMENT GIVES MONEY TO MY SON AND ME EVERY month—survivors' benefits. The amount is different for each survivor. The government has a magic calculation and it depends on how much income tax your deceased one paid. My son could receive the money until he was eighteen, and I could also receive money until he was sixteen. When I told my mother how much they were giving each of us, she said, "How lucky! That's the starting salary of a Japanese junior high school graduate. But for you without working. You're like a celebrity."

I worked just enough hours at a Japanese language preschool to still qualify for PG&E discount, Internet Essentials, free school meals, and free Medicaid. I heard, in America, unless you are on Medi-Cal, riding in an ambulance costs money. I was always afraid about getting in a car accident, being sent to a hospital by ambulance, and going bankrupt. How could I refuse the service if I was in a coma? I would have to wear a dog tag or a T-shirt, saying, *Do not call for an ambulance. I choose to die rather than go broke.*

Every spring after we moved back to San Francisco, my mother-in-law came to visit us. Passover, Alex's birthday, snow in Boston, and her back pain all occurred in one month—a perfect time for her to escape from New England.

"I think I could stay with you for two months or a whole winter, even. We get along so well, don't we?" Bubbe said.

"The gas is going up," I said, pointing out the price outside. We were driving to Ross, again, to exchange the sandals she'd bought for a memory foam pillow.

"I really need new sandals. The last time I bought a pair of sandals was five years ago and I think I deserve a new pair," she said the first day she arrived at my house, so I took her to Ross the next day. Just less than three days later, she decided that she wanted to return the sandals because with that money she could buy me a pillow. "I decided you deserve a new pillow. I'm going to buy you a memory foam. I'll use it while I'm here so it's for me. You don't have to feel bad about spending my money."

My mother-in-law slept in my bed and I slept on my couch. I made a nice thick pillow for her the way she preferred, doubling two in one. I was proud of myself for recycling old flat pillows, but when I told her about it, Bubbe said, "Oy! You're as bad as my ex-husband."

*Deserve*. I tried to recall the translation of this English word to Japanese, but I couldn't. In Japan, we don't think about what we are entitled to on a daily basis. Here in the U.S., it's all about claiming your needs and rights. No one cares about you unless you speak up for yourself. People here need to do that to survive, I learned. But what I was really thinking about at the moment was the cost of gasoline. My budget for gas was two fill-ups per month. The way things were going with Bubbe, I would be filling the tank three times.

"Can you stop by a drive-through? I need a drink," she said.

I knew this was coming.

"Don't worry, Bubbe. I brought a water bottle. I even put in ice cubes," I said, holding the bottle in one hand and keeping the other on the wheel.

"Thank you, but I need iced tea with artificial sweetener. You know my medication dries out my mouth. I cannot have sugar, but the sweetener helps the liquid stick to my mouth."

I had no idea what she was talking about, about the artificial sweetener being a glue to her mouth, but I knew I couldn't win. I drove to McDonald's.

The line extended from the parking lot into the street.

"It's crowded, Bubbe. Do you really need to have their iced tea? Can I run to the Safeway next to the Ross and get you a Diet Coke?"

"No, that's ridiculous! I can't make you work like that."

Bubbe was generous. Once when we were visiting her in Massachusetts, a young plumber came to fix her toilet. It was Christmas Eve. Outside it was snowing and beautiful. Of course, that didn't matter to me or Bubbe. We didn't celebrate Christmas and needed a working toilet, but the plumber boy wasn't Jewish, and he had just broken up with his girlfriend. While he fixed the toilet, I heard him talking to Bubbe, who was watching TV in her bedroom, across from the bathroom, about his girlfriend and what a stupid man he was to have let her go. The boy was nice. He also hung Bubbe's grandfather's painting in the living room and rearranged the sofas, both things Bubbe couldn't do by herself.

After he completed Bubbe's favors, she called him into her bedroom and gave him a bottle of water and a banana. *You are not stupid. She made a mistake to let go of such a nice boy like you,* I heard her say. I glanced at Bubbe's room on my way to the toilet. The boy sat by the edge of Bubbe's bed and started talking about his hardworking father and the mother who left him when he was three.

*I didn't have a good role model. I don't understand women. I may be chasing my mother's shadow. I'm haunted by her ghost.*

*You are young and kind. You'll find a nice girl, find a Jewish girl, I'm telling you they will take care of you.*

Bubbe lived in an income-based senior housing apartment and the building had its own plumber. The boy was paid a salary. He didn't have to kill time to get paid. The boy's voice, which was so soft, almost whispering, as if he was trying to suppress his emotion, and Bubbe's crisp, affirming words mixed with nods leaked from her bedroom. I thought how lucky to have a mother-in-law who could care about a stranger enough to invite him into her bedroom for water and a banana.

"Kyoko, do you have ten dollars?" Bubbe came out of her bedroom when the boy went to the bathroom.

"I do but why?"

"Ron is sad. He has no girlfriend. We should give him some money."

"But isn't he getting paid from the building?"

"He is. I'm giving him extra so he can buy chocolate for himself. It's Christmas. He needs something to cheer him up."

That moment, I knew Bubbe was the most generous person I've ever met. She literally went above and beyond to give money to a stranger.

"Here, take this." Bubbe wrapped the boy's hand with her two hands. "It's not that much. Come back here anytime if you need some-one to talk."

Her kindness extended to someone else's child, so you could only imagine how she was to me. Bubbe always came to visit us with two suitcases: one packed with her clothes and another filled with Joyva raspberry jelly rings, Streit's egg matzo boxes, and Manischewitz's ge-filte fish in a jar. With her, we could have Passover every spring.

I went grocery shopping once a week and I only bought what was on my list. The list didn't change much, and I always went to the same grocery store, so I memorized the prices. Sixty dollars every week and two hundred fifty for the month was my budget.

This year, I even implemented a new toilet rule to help in the drought, but really to save on my water bill. When it was only me and Alex in the house, we waited to flush for three pees or for one poop. Alex couldn't be happier. He even asked me if he could skip wiping his butt after number two. I told him that would not save us water since I would have to hand wash his underwear with running water before I put them into the laundry. Boys, they always look for shortcuts to their bathroom rituals—wiping butts, washing hands, and closing doors.

Bubbe was impressed.

"You are so frugal. You beat my ex-husband," she said.

I told her, since I didn't want her to feel uncomfortable, I would put the ritual on hold. She thanked me but also begged me not to disclose this routine to anyone besides her.

If I was called minimalist, Bubbe would be called maximalist. While I felt accomplished to see the empty fridge at the end of week, Bubbe felt depressed. It reminded her of the Great Depression.

"Kyoko, groceries are on me. I'm going to cook extra and fill your freezer, so you and Alex have food for a while." This was her mission every year.

I appreciated her kindness but what I was really worried about was the extra time I had to spend at the grocery store several times a week, as well as trips to McDonald's, Ross, and Peet's Coffee for snack breaks during shopping trips because Bubbe said, *How could you do the grocery shopping when you are hungry?* I didn't need her to stock up my freezer. I could support Alex and myself with $250 a month. I'd done this for many years without anyone's help. I could survive without her. Besides, we ate different food. Bubbe liked honey nut

Cheerios with vanilla almond milk, cherry tomatoes with hummus, Swiss cheese on top of Ritz crackers, Diet Coke, and Crystal Light peach iced tea. Alex and I ate miso soup, rice, fruit, and cucumbers, and drank water, milk, and green tea. If she could just buy her own food, we could keep the shopping trip to once a week. Besides, she kept forgetting her debit card PIN number or kept remembering the wrong number. "It's hard to remember things at my age as you can see. Remind me to pay you back, please," she would say in the car on the way home. She always paid me back if I mentioned it, but I felt bad for reminding her so often, so I began covering the cost. I already knew I would be the one paying for the memory foam pillow today.

Alex needed new soccer cleats, registration for the team cost eighty dollars, and the class potluck was just three weeks away. I saved money for these extra expenses in advance in a savings account named "annual expense." But I'd been withdrawing money from it for the last two weeks. Soon, I would have to create an account named "annual Bubbe expense" and be even more frugal. If I was worrying about sending Alex to his soccer team next month, how could I send him to college? Bubbe staying two months? The entire winter? I would go bankrupt. Besides, the money wasn't really *my* money. The government gave my husband's Social Security to me to take care of my son, not me. The pillow wasn't for Alex.

"I'm going to turn off my engine. The line isn't going to move anytime soon," I said.

"It's hot. We'll melt. We can't turn off the air conditioner."

"It's not hot. I'm wearing a sweater and jacket."

"Keep that on and run the AC. No one wants to see me naked. You have no fat. You need to eat more, Kyoko. Stop eating miso and have some of my Ritz."

"I'm worried about the cost of gas, Bubbe."

"Don't you worry. I'll pay."

"No, it's okay. I'm doing fine without your help. I just can't take any unexpected expenses every time you come. The gas, water, electricity, nose spray, Noah's bagels . . . it costs me more when you come. My job at preschool is only part-time and minimum wage. I can't take this anymore."

The line at McDonald's finally moved up. I ordered one iced tea and asked for ice cubes in a separate cup. The cashier hesitated at first, but when Bubbe explained that where she lived, the two-cup rule was acceptable for seniors and she could get on the phone with the manager from her McDonald's if he needed proof, he gave up fighting.

"See, I told you it wasn't so long," Bubbe said.

"It was fifteen minutes. That's long enough to kill one redwood tree."

I dropped her off in front of Ross and drove in a circle until I found a parking spot. Bubbe had a hard time walking without a cane. These little extra drives added up. I jogged into the store, passed her from behind, and headed to the pillow section. By the time she was walking near the exchange line, I'd already grabbed the pillow and lined up to pay the difference. Bubbe joined me. She remembered her PIN number this time. She bought her memory foam pillow for me.

I ran back to my car, and when I saw Bubbe walking out of the store, I started my engine and drove up to the front of the store.

"Thank you, Kyoko. We're a good team. You know how much I appreciate you. Not many mothers-in-law can visit their daughters-in-law without their son. I hear so many of my friends complaining about their daughters-in-law. But not me. I want you to know I am so happy you are my daughter-in-law, no, my daughter."

I knew this wasn't the guilt trip she often used on her family. She was being sincere to me just as she'd promised when we lost Levi. No matter how painful it could be, she would speak her mind, and asked me to do the same. The regret, resentment, and shame would build a wall around you, she believed, and by telling the truth we would break the wall and unite.

"I don't get hurt easily. Just tell me what you want. If I don't like it, I won't do it. You and I are in this together," she said.

When the house went into foreclosure, Alex and I decided to live with my brother-in-law and his family in Massachusetts. I asked Bubbe if she could stay with us for a while because I was scared. I feared my mental state. Bubbe stayed with us until we moved back to San Francisco.

At night I would come to her room and sit on the edge of her bed, just like the plumber boy did. We watched whatever show she was watching and during the commercials, I told her how much I hated it there. I hated the cold winter and overpriced, unripe fruits. I told her I'd rather starve than eat her cooking.

When she tried to make me feel better, I bit back at her words with reasons to make myself feel worse. Maybe, by doing so, I could be excused from suffering another loss, of whom, I didn't know. Or I could prepare for the next tragedy. A survival instinct. The pain would be less if my mood already was at its lowest. I wanted to stay in the pit. I didn't want to feel better. I wanted not to go through the pain again.

After I had listed all the reasons why I should be punished, I'd tell her about being afraid about surviving in this country as a single immigrant mother but wanting to be independent at the same time. I told her how I felt guilty about depending on her or her family but couldn't muster up the courage to leave my brother-in-law's comfortable house and start over again.

"Go, Kyoko. Move back to San Francisco. No one lives with yourself but you. You must make yourself happy first. If it doesn't work out, you can always come back here. Ben would never refuse you and Alex, and even after Alex grows up, he would still take you in in a heartbeat. You know why? Because we're family. Do you understand?"

I still had Alex, and Bubbe still had three kids and their grandkids. We weren't technically alone, but when we sat on her bed together, we could feel alone together and when we were alone together, I felt maybe I could live on the other side of the country again, knowing she would always be here for me.

"What does the sign say?" Bubbe pointed to the vintage wooden sign. We were driving back to my house.

"That's a pie store. Someone brought a banana cream pie from the shop to a potluck once. They are pretty good," I said.

"Kyoko, can we go? Banana cream pie is my favorite pie. We *deserve* a piece of pie. I'll pay for both of us."

She was leaving in a week. One piece of pie wouldn't hurt my bank account at this point. Why not? I dropped her off in front of the store and went around to find a parking spot.

When I arrived at the store, Bubbe was already seated at a table.

She tried to give me her debit card, I waved my hands in front of me to gesture, *I got this.*

The pie cost seven dollars a piece. A piece.

I ordered one for Bubbe and got a glass of tap water for me.

"Where is yours, Kyoko?"

"I didn't want it."

"You love sweets. You are the only person who could refuse my chicken soup to save room for chocolate. You finished the five boxes of raspberry Joyva jelly in three days. I know you. Please let me buy a piece of pie for you."

"No, I'm fine."

"You're lying. How can I eat this without you? I want to remember this moment with you. That's why I asked to stop for pie."

"I don't want to spend money for myself, and I don't want *you* to spend money on me. It's not worth it. I'd rather you save money for Alex. He will need money for his Bar Mitzvah. I'm like dirt, a pest, or a leech to this country."

And to Levi, I wanted to tell Bubbe. I was a leech to him and that was the reason why he secretly took out a credit card under my name and left debt, and no life insurance. But I didn't dare to say that to her. This is one emotion I'll take to my grave.

"What are you talking about, Kyoko?" Bubbe asked.

"The government gives me money to take care of Alex. It's his money. I thought I would feel independent if I lived alone in San Francisco, but I'm still depending on someone: my son and the government," I said.

Bubbe stood up, went to the cashier, and returned to her seat. "Forks are free for use. We share." She pushed the plate of pie in front of me.

"Listen, Kyoko. Because so many kids lost their fathers in World War Two, women couldn't support their kids and gave them away to orphanages. It's more economical to give money to widows and widowers to raise their children than to spend money for orphanages. The U.S. government gives you money for that reason. So, you have every right to spend money for this pie," she continued. "Without a happy mother, there will be no happy kid. I don't understand where you got the idea of being a burden to this country, but let me tell you this. I marched for women's rights in the sixties, Levi on my back and Ben in the stroller. Don't waste our effort."

In front of us, an untouched piece of banana cream pie and two silver forks sat. My tears fogged my view of the family with a small child, the couple, and the store worker who wiped tables hurriedly behind Bubbe. In this big world, Bubbe and I looked like the center of the story.

"The U.S. government doesn't love you, but they want you to live, and having pie with your mother-in-law is living. You're cheap, obsessive, and sometimes sickly paranoid. But it's not hard to love you. Ben, Paula, Laura, me, and even Zaydeh—no one is obligated to love you, we do because we want to. Don't run away from love, Kyoko. Don't run away from it. And even if everyone in this world goes against you, including yourself, I won't. I promised Levi at his grave, I'll always be there for you, so get a grip, you'll never get rid of me. When I die, Ben will figure out a way to preserve my head. I'll be a talking head. For God's sake, half of my body is already made of titanium, I might as well be without a body."

A store worker came with an extra plate.

Bubbe cut the piece of pie exactly in half and pushed the second plate to me. "No cheating, Kyoko," she said.

After we finished eating, I quickly went out to get my car and cried a little more. Levi might not have loved me, but he left me a person who would never stop loving me.

It took a few minutes before I started driving. Bubbe waited for me as she always had done, in front of the store.

"See, Kyoko. We get along so well. You drive yourself crazy and I make you feel better. I'm going to come for two months next year."

I didn't respond.

"What do you say, Kyoko?"

"You're the best thing Levi left me, but I don't think I can handle you for eight weeks. Maybe two weeks, no, ten days is all I can take, to be honest. I've been thrown out of my own rhythm, and I want my bed and the new pillow back."

"I cannot believe this. After my long, outstanding speech, you're kicking me out."

We passed the same gas station by my house. The gas had gone up again!

I said, "Bubbe, the gas just went up ten cents since we passed by three hours ago."

Bubbe laughed and patted my thigh. "This is why I love you."

# A Parent's Blessing

BAR MITZVAH SPEECH DRAFT 1

A year ago, when we started the Bar Mitzvah process, Alex said to me, "Mom, you can embarrass me all you want but don't give a boring blessing, but since you are already boring, all you need to do is not to be yourself." This brief exchange captures the Alex that we all love. Authentic, very comfortable to be himself, and committed to enjoying every moment of his life, even his mother's blessing. In response to your request, Alex, I'm going to tell you a story, and it's about your father, our wedding, and Bubbe. And you know when Bubbe and your father are in the story, things aren't going to be the way you expect.

Your father, Bubbe, and I were sitting at the table and planning for our Boston wedding. Bubbe said, "Kyoko, this is your night, you can have anything you want." I said, "Nothing." And she said, "That's not the correct answer. What do you want for your wedding?" I said, "Then, something very, very, very small. Just family and dinner." Bubbe said, "That's an excellent idea. Levi, we're having a small wedding." This is a family that could have a heated discussion all day long about where to go for dinner. I couldn't believe my wish had been granted so easily.

As the date neared, Bubbe began to ask me questions. "Kyoko, I think the tablecloth should be gold. It's elegant and doesn't show the mess as much. But it's your wedding, I want to make sure you like my idea." I said, "Anything is fine as long as it's small." "Kyoko, I ordered a wedding cake from Konditor Meister, the best pastry store in Massachusetts. But I want to make sure." I'd go, "That's great. As long as it's a small wedding." "Kyoko, my dear friend is a floral designer. He is making a bouquet for you and a centerpiece for each table." I thought, *Centerpiece for each table? For a small wedding, that's odd*. Around the same time, I also noticed on your father's desk, there was a pile of invitation cards. Soon he started talking about hiring a band, the photographer, and the open bar. By then I was so entertained by this, this mother-and-son combo struggling to compress the wedding, which seemed to be the only thing they didn't know how to do.

The day came, the ceremony was small, just with immediate family. But when I walked into the hall next to the ceremony room, I saw over sixty people seated. There was the gold tablecloth that Bubbe was talking about, the centerpiece flower on each table that Bubbe was talking about, and the tall wedding cake, the size of which Bubbe hadn't mentioned. And among the people, I saw Don, your father's childhood friend; Richie, the junkyard owner; Steve, the nightclub bouncer...I asked your father, "What happened to the family wedding?" His answer was "They're all family to me." That was my favorite thing about your father. Until then, family to me was my mother, father, and my brother. Just four. And that was plenty for me. But after I met your father my definition of family expanded. And when my definition of family expanded, my capacity for love expanded as well. And when the capacity for love expands, so does life itself.

The story leads to your life, now and today at your Bar Mitzvah. Now I'm going to be boring because it's me talking.

Because your father was so good at initiating friendship and I wasn't, when we lost your father, I was worried that you'd be alone. But looking at everyone here, I know I have nothing to worry about.

Alex, I want you to take a moment to look at each face in the audience.

They're here today because they want to be. You were only two years old when we returned to San Francisco, and we knew almost no one. Alex, you built your community from nothing to this.

Status, money, and any visible achievement might lead you to a comfortable lifestyle and chip away some fear for the future, but friends and family make your life. Meeting people is the greatest gift, but it solely happens by luck. However, keeping the relationship going is done by effort. What you see in front of you is not pure luck. It's you who created this. And, you know from the story I just told you this is what your father valued the most.

Without you, none of the people would be here today. That means if it wasn't for you, I wouldn't have any of my friends. Alex, you not only built a life for yourself, but for me. For this, I'm still searching for how to say thank you.

I can honestly say that your life is the life I wish for every child to experience. Keep building the life you can love. You have no obligation to make anyone or even me happy or proud. You must know, loving yourself has nothing to do with being selfish or unempathetic. So don't sell your life to anyone.

Everyone, thank you for raising Alex with me. He would not be who he is if one of you were missing from his life. I say this sincerely. As he is becoming a young man, you know you can also start counting on him. When you need someone, he will be there for you as you have been there for him.

Alex, take a good look at everyone one more time. They are the life that you built for yourself. You can forget everything I said, but remember just one thing. At age thirteen, you had everything you needed.

# An Infant Confession

I WATCHED THEIR BABY FALL ASLEEP IN MY ARMS. A HALF HOUR AGO he woke up crying, so I gave him a bottle, walked him around their living room, and sang an improvised lullaby. The baby smelled good, like all newborn babies do, like milk, with the added scent of their house. I'd been trying to figure out where the smell came from ever since I became his older sister's babysitter. I guessed either essential oil or laundry detergent. I refused to ask his parents because even if I knew what it was, it would be impossible to create the exact scent in my house. The scent must evolve with each life in the household. I wondered if my son and I too had created a distinctive smell.

The baby's father used to be my professor. He and his family lived only five blocks from me. They kept their house as if they had just moved in: books, bills, take-out food, and dog leashes everywhere. No wonder my professor couldn't find his students' papers.

Despite the fact that no one could deny his talent as a writer and a teacher, and his class was always filled as soon as registration opened, some complained about his absentmindedness and unpredictability. He often double-booked meetings and was always late. I embraced his inconsistency and forgetfulness as part of his charm but some of my classmates told me he did this on purpose to keep us away from him. There was one girl who even cried because he forgot about their meeting. She said that he didn't care about us at all. I was puzzled by her comment because I already knew he didn't care about us.

The truth was that I enrolled in the creative writing program because they didn't require a GRE, unlike the English department. Tutors fixed my English while I was in my four-year college. I followed their red marks and retyped my essays just to pass the classes. I still had no idea when I needed to add commas or when to use "a" instead of "the." *What would it be like to really understand this language? If I could write like native speakers, would I finally feel like I belong here?* I wanted to know.

Soon, I realized people in the program were above the grammar. They broke the grammar rules and made up words. They could because they had mastered the rules of English.

But my professor didn't care about my grammar. He also didn't care about me. What he cared about were our stories. That was exactly why I liked him. I didn't have to explain my life to him. He only wanted to know about the people in my stories. In his class, I wasn't confined by my body. If my stories failed to move people, I could change the characters or give them up. I fell in love with the freedom.

He invited me to work on his various projects, and after I graduated from the program, he asked me to be his daughter's babysitter. I spent all my energy loving his daughter when she was with me. The daughter and my son were six years apart. The three of us played charades, Mouse Trap, and The Game of Life together. The two fought over the rules and who was the winner of the game just like I imagined siblings would fight. His daughter and I made Japanese flip-card books and shadow puppets, and recorded stories we had improvised. She hated vegetables and fruit but my avocado sushi she ate more than any adult I knew could eat. We baked gluten-free cake for her mother. The frosting was made of fish eyeballs, I told her, and her already big eyes got even bigger, then she immediately squinted her eyes like a detective would do and said, "Are you sure?" In my car, I keep my professor's house key, and my backseat has numerous stains from his dog's drool. I know his best friend's name and how his wife forges his signature emphasizing "P" and "F" to write a check for me. But we aren't close. We never have had dinner together, not even a casual chat except to talk about my stories, his project, or his kids, and that's the way I prefer us to be.

In my arms, my professor's baby snored and smiled simultaneously. Then, I heard the door unlock, followed by a "Hello?"—his wife, Tea's, bright voice coming into the house. She found me on the sofa, the same spot I had been in when she left, and she told me, "You didn't have to hold him the whole time." I noticed her baby had started to wiggle in my arms. He made a raisin face, the face he would always make before he burst into crying. "You're just fine! You smell food, don't you?" I passed him to Tea, and she went into her bedroom. "I'll start from the painting on the wall," I said, and she shouted, "That would be awesome! I'll be right there."

The family was moving to Africa for a year, and then to New Hampshire. Tea had asked me to help them pack. Their second child had just been born. They needed a hand.

With a big smile, Tea said, "Our house is a mess!" The vintage salt and pepper shakers, a pig ceramic statue, which seemed to have no purpose except to be an extra obstacle on the kitchen shelf to dust . . . things I'd never keep in my house, Tea brought them to me and I wrapped them individually like I'd wrap a gift. She showed me a portrait of her drawn by one of her ex-boyfriends. She showed me her photo album, a picture of her and her brother on a boat when she was a three-year-old. She showed me a sepia-colored photograph of my professor with his brother in the woods when he was still a young boy. "I'm making progress," Tea said, looking around the living room. "I don't know about Poe. That's his problem." She circled her finger around the bookshelf above the fireplace.

Leaving several small paintings on the sofa to pack later, we moved into the kitchen to wrap my professor's mug collection. She told me he had a habit of pilfering mugs every place he visited. We found a mug with a Mission Pie logo, a mug from a Lake Tahoe lodge with a saucer, and cheap Ikea mugs from Charlie's Cafe. She imitated his expression the moment he turned into a thief. "He is a strange person," she said. The way she said it contained so much love for him that my heart ached. Their messy house was full of life, and as I packed their lives into boxes, I felt like I was part of their family.

I wrapped the rest of the photographs and paintings in their living room. I heard the door open and without a "Hello" or "I'm home," my professor came upstairs. *How did it go?* Tea asked. He was coming home after the presentation about Africa at his daughter's school. *You wouldn't believe how smart these five years olds are!* he said to her. *They know every single animal in Africa. I mean not just a giraffe, a zebra, a lion but a wildebeest and all that.* He picked up the portrait done by Tea's ex-boyfriend, and mussing his hair he said to me, "This will be one of the unspoken family legacies, don't you think?" As though I had just appeared in his living room, he asked me, "How is it going?"

"We made progress but your books . . ." And I circled my finger around the bookshelf above the fireplace.

"Oh, I can do that now," he said, and he started pulling all his books out. "I mean, I don't need them, right? Look at this, it's too much."

I watched him making two piles—for "keep" and "donate." In between making these piles, he asked me, "I'm doing these podcasts with Erika, do you want to help edit them?"

"Sure, I've never edited audio . . ."

"But you can learn. Yes?"

"Yes."

"You can edit, right?"

"Right, I can edit," I said.

He did this dance where he carried the "donate" pile to the hallway and took several books out from the pile and put some back on the shelf. I followed the "donate" stack and picked up the book on the top, and on the front page, I found my professor's scribblings trying to come up with a praise quote for his author friend. I tucked the book in my purse, and the rest I packed into two paper bags just for me.

It took at least ten minutes for my professor to leave the house. *Where are my keys?* he asked and Tea answered, *The last time I saw them they were on the table.* Then he asked her again, *How about my backpack? It's right in front of you, on the couch,* she answered. *Do you know where the paper I was carrying this morning is? You left with it this morning.* He walked around his house as he collected his missing objects. He picked up a framed photograph that I had laid on the couch to pack. *Oh, this is a great picture, we have to keep that,* he said and placed it on the floor.

He finally left the house, saying he was taking his bike. After we heard the door shut, Tea looked at me and said, "It's like having three kids!" We both smiled.

We packed some more boxes, then it was time for Tea to pick her daughter up from school for her piano lesson. She passed me her son. "How would we live without you?" she said. *Vice versa,* I wanted to say, but instead, I nodded and grabbed the bags of "donate" books.

Outside, my professor had just returned from whatever errand he was running and was getting into his car. "I should have taken my car instead," he said when he saw me with his baby son and bags of books.

"Why don't I give you a ride?" he said.

"It's only five blocks away, I'm fine."

"Okay," he said and asked me, "Are you coming to Charlie's to-night? I'm doing a reading and Paul is singing. I mean it's kind of silly but . . ."

"Yes, I'll be there."

"And tomorrow? Birthday party? We'll have a jumping castle. I'm not sure if Alex will jump with a bunch of five-year-olds."

"He wouldn't miss it for his life," I said.

"And the Haiti project."

"Yes, I will go over it again."

"Are you sure you don't need a ride?"

"Yes, I'm fine," I said, and he opened the car door and moved his books to the backseat.

"So, see you tonight?"

"And tomorrow and yesterday."

He smiled, mussing his hair, and I smiled too.

When his car turned the corner of Precita Avenue, I embraced his baby through the baby carrier. I whispered to him, "I love you so much." The weight of the paper bags hindered me from continuing to embrace him but I didn't let go of either the books or the baby. I kissed the sleeping baby and smelled his neck. "I love you. I love you. I love you," I repeated. He was only a few weeks old. He couldn't understand what I said but I know he felt it and will keep it to himself.

# I Heard My Son Kissing a Girl

ON OSCAR NIGHT, I HEARD MY SON KISSING A GIRL. HE WAS FIFTEEN years old and this was the first time he had brought a girl to our place. He told me at the dinner table prior to the kissing incident that they were watching *Rango* in his room. Did the cartoon involve a lot of kissing? Maybe, but I couldn't remember, so I tried to listen to them to figure out whether the sound was from the screen or from them. Each time I heard the pecking sound, it became more real and I put together the thread of their conversation. *Are you okay?* said my son. *Yes, yes. I'm fine*, said the girl.

Between witnessing the first time a Korean movie won best picture and a pit-bull-size raccoon trespassing on our front porch, I texted my son, who was two feet away, just on the other side of the wall. *Are you guys ok? There is a giant raccoon outside. Do you guys want to see it?* No answer. The pecking sound (now I'm convinced it was) kept leaking through his wall. Of course, they were more than okay, but I didn't know what else to say or not to say. I would have been more prepared if he had told me she was his girlfriend. I could have told him our house rule, *Someone has to be home when you bring a girl, if you do things you don't want me to see or hear then don't,* and, and . . . what?

We lived in San Francisco in a hundred-year-old, two-story house with housemates. The layout of the house allowed our housemates and us to have our privacy. We shared a garage, kitchen, backyard, and laundry room. The sunroom in the back and the entire second floor, two bedrooms and a shower and toilet, were my housemates' space, and a living room and one huge bedroom with a bath and toilet on the first floor were our space. I divided the huge bedroom into two bedrooms when my son was six. We used two bookcases that my first housemates had left to create two-thirds of the boundary, and we covered the space above them with Ikea curtains. We didn't build a wall between us.

It's a miracle that we could still afford to rent a place in this city. Levi had owned his house on this same street, but he died during the rise of the housing market crisis and the house went into foreclosure. It was a miracle that we found a rental on the same street and that my son grew up with the same neighbors and friends. Our landlord, a retired firefighter, a man of few words, never raised our rent until four years ago, and every time he did, he said, "I'm so sorry that I have to do this to you." There were times when I couldn't find new housemates, but he didn't charge me the full house rent. He said, "Just pay what you've always paid. You are a single mother. Focus on raising your son."

Families we collected over the years became Alex's fathers, mothers, aunts, and uncles, and my best friends. They watched Alex while I went to school at night. They invited us over for dinners, camping trips, and into their phone plans. It's a miracle to be able to feel the entire city helping to bring up one child. My son's friends didn't tease him about his living situation. On the contrary, one boy begged his mom to find a housemate and get rid of his brother. This was back when they were still in third grade. The boy who wanted to give away his brother still came to have a sleepover, and I often found him in our living room on the weekends, now six foot two, so he couldn't fit on our couch to sleep. He slept on a giant beanbag, half of his body hanging on the floor and my son on the couch sleeping, curled in a ball. Whether your parents owned a Tesla, had a vacation house in Tahoe, or lived with housemates, kids didn't care. They saw each other as they were. The things I saw on the TV show—the social hierarchy, rich kids looking down on poor kids, or poor kids feeling ashamed of their parents—they weren't our reality. So our nonexistent wall had never been a problem to us . . . until this Oscar night.

The girl's mother came to pick her up at a quarter after ten.

The mother asked her, "Did you have fun?"

The girl said, "Yes."

The mother and daughter left with big smiles.

My son came to the living room looking at his phone. He'd just read my text. He smiled and shook his head, "Yes, we're okay."

"I could hear you guys and I didn't know what to do. Is she your girlfriend?"

"Yes."

"I see."

I couldn't recall what kind of conversation led us to sit down on the couch across from each other. All I remember was asking him, "Are you guys going to have sex? Do you have a condom?"

He answered, "No, I'm not going to. I'm only fifteen. I don't want to have a baby. We've had sex education, not just once but multiple times. If I have a concern, we have a school counselor for that."

I told him that it's better to be safe than sorry so if he needed a condom, I'd buy it. If he didn't want me to, he could always ask Sam's dad, Walter's dad, or any of his fathers. I wanted him to know he could speak to me or any of us.

"I know, Mom. Please. Can you just stop?" he said and left to take a shower. I could see he was getting upset. I knew I had failed at our first *talk* and possibly I had lost the chance for it forever. I sat on the couch while he took a shower thinking about what had happened to my ideal parent image, that I would be a parent who listens to her child, be open to his freedom, and trust his answer. So, I decided to leave a box of condoms in his room without mentioning it. Did condoms have a size? I didn't know. If they did, what size would I need to get for him?

When he came out of the bathroom, Alex said, "I know you're worried and I'm glad that you spoke to me. I got upset because you began to rumble the same line over and over. I've already heard about sex and protection so many times from so many people."

I told him I was happy that he was with her, especially knowing he had asked her out back in September, and she'd told him she was too busy at the time. He smiled and we said good night and went to sleep. *The talk* was done. *Good, we made a verbal contract,* I thought.

I worried about everything. I worried if he could make friends, if I could feed him in this city, if I could retain my job, if I could help with his English homework, and if I could behave well enough to be accepted by his community. But with each worry I had, his life proved they were only my fears. He was much more resilient and so was I.

There was one more worry, which I had not resolved. I had never had a serious, committed relationship after Levi died. This was not a sacrifice. I wasn't worried that my love life would ruin my son's life. I was worried about spending money. I didn't want to spend money on a dating site, transportation to a meeting spot, activities a date and I might be doing together, birthday cards for him, birth control pills, and other miscellaneous expenses that would come with having another person in my life. I also didn't want anyone to pay for my portion. I was now an independent woman, unlike when I was married to Levi, when I had to depend on him for my survival. My life was already full of love with people and with the community we were involved in. I didn't need any more love.

Could a parent without romance teach a child how to love? How could Alex learn to care for his girlfriend if I failed to show him what a couple should look like? So many novels and movies were born out of passion, and I knew loving someone was never a waste of time even if it only lasted three weeks. I knew it in my head, and sometimes I wanted to hire someone to be my boyfriend once a month so I could show my son that love was the greatest thing a human could experience. But I couldn't. I loved my life and I hated spending money.

The following week, Alex acted the same as before *that* night. He let me hug him, and some mornings he came to my bed to lie next to me. At dinner, we spoke a bit about his girlfriend and her overweight Chihuahua mix in the midst of conversation about his schoolwork and the volleyball team. But I was still consumed by that night. Alex moved on from the subject and I couldn't.

There was a ninth-grade parent meeting on Thursday night before the school play. After the meeting, I went to introduce myself to Alex's counselor and speak about his passion for history but really to seek her advice about my son's love life. "Yes, AP U.S. history sounds great. What I want to ask you about is that he has a girlfriend now. Will they have sex?" I asked.

She, with a serious look, said, "I cannot answer yes or no. But they are learning about protection and consent. You can set a house rule, speak with her parents, and ask him to inform you where he is."

I asked her if it was common in this country for fifteen-year-olds to kiss, and she said it was. She also told me, in a pitying tone, that it would only get harder from here.

Right after we said goodbye, she held my hand and said, "You must know your son is a great kid. He's friends with everyone and cares for them all. Really cares. That's a gift. I'm not just saying this to make you feel better. I want you to know how special that is!"

At the play, my son instructed me to sit in the front row, alone. I turned my head to the back. In the dim light, I spotted the shadow of his girlfriend's head leaning on his shoulder. They seemed so comfortable with each other.

Who had told him that lending your shoulder makes others relax?

I didn't have any memory of being loved by men. I remembered I had been loved, but I couldn't remember what it felt like. It wasn't as dramatic as a hole in my heart or my memory having been blocked out by a traumatic experience. My past must have existed because of what was born.

At night, when I was alone in the kitchen, I often listened to its buzz while I brought the corner of the fridge into focus. As I sat looking at the corner, my mind time-traveled to seventeen years ago with Levi. The diner that served the large blueberry pancakes, the heated conversation about our ideal society (back then I was into a barter-based society), the desire to be open to someone and the wish to find a person who would be my soul mate. Our coffee had gotten cold—the sign of enthusiastic discussion. We'd forgotten the time and space. I remembered the sensation, but this wasn't my emotion because I didn't taste it. Buzz, buzz, buzz. What's so noble about loving someone anyway?

"What's wrong with having sex?" my ex-roommate number 3 asked. Mi Cha and I were at a sake bar a few blocks from my house, owned by an elderly Japanese couple. Mi Cha had recently discovered a wonderful American TV show called *Cheers* and suggested I should find a go-to bar but with the twist of an owner who could act like a therapist so that I could prepare for the empty nest.

"Getting pregnant and having baby at a fifteen," I answered. "People who have a child at a young age live in poverty. It's a guarantee for suffering. Why do you dive into a situation that's already a clear tragedy? Can you imagine the dream your child has to give up to raise his child? I don't want to see him regret his life and blame the kid for it. Passion does not raise children. Planning does."

I could have gone on more but I stopped.

"So, if they don't get pregnant, you're okay with them having sex as much as they want?"

"Oh yes, all day, every day! In fact they should explore what gives them pleasure when they are still young. Both are equally naïve about love. Every touch and whisper feels like a new discovery. We don't get that kind of joy once we're under the pressure of having a roof over our heads. Sex becomes body maintenance, like eating fiber and going to the bathroom."

"Or a business transaction."

"I love sex being a business transaction, Mi Cha! Except once we become accustomed to American culture and we begin to voice ourselves, 'more free time, less sex,' husbands travel to find another young, naïve woman who dreams to live in America. Or, they evaporate suddenly and we find them in Japan with another woman. That happened to my friends Kotomi, Maki, and Yoshi. Yoshi told her husband she wanted to focus on raising their kids rather than spending time in bed with him. He said she didn't love him anymore and he took off next day. Poof! Just like that. A few months later, he sends a divorce paper from Japan. The husband traveled to Japan and brought back a woman who was ten years younger than Yoshi. Can you believe he crossed the sea, to her home country, to *pick* another wife?"

"My friend has sex with her husband when she wants a new handbag."

"Why can't a husband have an affair with someone and leave us alone, and just give us money to take care of our children? For us, Asian wives, family comes first and sex . . . not even on the list! But when we tell that to a therapist here, they say it's our fault that we neglect the couple part. The *couple* part? People in this country are so obsessed with being a couple!"

"Asian immigrant. Because we can't speak for Asian American wives. Asian immigrant wives. Or do we say immigrant Asian wives?"

"Don't ask me. I'm Japanese. My English is as bad as yours. Hey, Mr. Sasaki, does 'immigrant' come before or after 'Asian'?" I asked the couple who owned the bar in Japanese.

"We were dancers who made a life in America by serving sake and fake sushi. We didn't need much English," the husband said in Japanese. "But I tell you, the other day, I was watching this Japanese TV program. The show asks ordinary people to show inside their house. They visited a young couple's house and found out that this couple had five kids. They had an accident pregnancy when they were fifteen but decided to have the child. You'll think their stories are packed with suffering. No, the opposite. Full of joy. They had no financial help so they struggled but their parents welcomed their decisions with their whole heart. No questions asked. You see, a problem becomes the problem when you see the incident as a problem. And the best kind of happiness is the one that happens without planning. Let it unfold. You should watch the TV program. It made this old man cry."

"You cry for everything," the wife said. "You cried with a video clip of a cat giving birth to six kittens. You cried when our granddaughter played an awful violin at the recital. But yes, the best joy comes from an accident. We fled to America because my father threatened him with a Japanese sword when we asked his permission for marriage. My father was a famous sword master and wanted me to marry his apprentice. The worst thing my father had ever done to us brought the best outcome."

We left after three sakes. Mi Cha paid for my drinks. I asked the bar owners if they could accept me staying at the counter with one cup of sake next time and as an exchange, I would do dishes for them. I would leave, of course, once the bar got busy. They laughed and said yes. If every single seat were taken, they would consider me good fortune and keep me in the corner forever because it had never happened in the last twenty-five years.

"How long will it take you to forgive Levi?" Mi Cha asked. We were just passing Precita Park. Sake had warmed us, and we decided to take a detour to my house. We were tipsy.

"What do you mean?"

"You don't talk about him and it's as if he never existed. You've told me how he died and about him as Alex's dad but not as a man you loved."

Love? I was stuck with the word, again. I've examined, analyzed, and dissected the word, and come to a conclusion: The definition would be more precise if we replaced the word with "attachment," "survival instinct," "loneliness," "excuse," or "infatuation." "Love" is a cheap, vague, lazy, overrated word that allows us to escape from any situation.

"Nothing to forgive him for because there is nothing he did wrong. Well, except that he had no life insurance. I don't care if Buddha tells me the source of all suffering of humankind comes from attachment, I'm going to attach, glue, fuse, embrace to the life insurance!"

"Hear, hear! No life insurance, unthinkable."

"Yes, if the sex becomes a business transaction for couple, financial security should come with it."

"Right! Right! But, Kyoko, you know, dead people don't get hurt. Only alive ones do."

The Japanese TV show that Mr. Sasaki suggested showed the house of a couple in their thirties. They lived with five children in a three-bedroom single-family house, a small distance away from Tokyo. The mother showed the camera crew around the house. *The laundry machine runs in the morning and at night. There is always someone taking a bath. Look at this place, it's like a steam room.* The camera shot the edge of the shower door. The black mold stained the silicone sealant. *Don't show the mold on the TV, it's embarrassing,* said her daughter. The mother laughed while her daughter giggled, hiding behind her. Despite the number of people living in the house, the living room was well organized and clean. Two refrigerators were occupied in the kitchen, and a son and another daughter were cooking curry rice. The son sliced onions and the daughter sautéed them with carrots and meat. Another giggled from shyness about their showing their cooking skill on a national TV show. The reporter asked the eldest daughter, who was twenty, *Don't you want to have your own place? I thought about it a bit when I was sixteen but no,* she said, *they are like friends who will never leave me no matter what, including my parents.* The reporter asked the eldest son, who was nineteen, *Don't you wish to have privacy? Well, this is all I know,* he said, and he shrugged. The reporter became even more aggressive with the parents and asked, *Might you have been able to do things you wanted to do if you didn't have a child so early?* The father scratched his head and said, *We couldn't wait to get married. By the time we were legally allowed to marry at eighteen years old, we had three children. My wife and I literally skipped our way to the city hall. It was hard to raise five with a high school diploma. My wife quit school and we've borrowed money from loan sharks. But I cannot think of any other life besides this.* At the end of the show, they shot the mother and the youngest son dancing along to music on the smartphone, then switched to the dining scene, where some kids ate standing and others sat on the sofa while the mother ate sitting on a stool. They all found their place in one room. "Imagine" by John Lennon began to play, and the screen and music slowly faded out as the show ended.

*Friends who never leave you no matter what. I wish I could give siblings to Alex,* I thought. The bar owner was right, every incident has two sides.

Even if his girlfriend and Alex got pregnant, and decided to keep their baby, it was possible that this could turn out to be the best event in their lives rather than the worst. Even for me, it would be an opportunity to hold a baby again. They would need help while they were in school. I could help! I might become good friends with her parents, and we could be a family of six. I'm still young. If things work out, I might be alive for their great-grandchild.

I began to see a bright future. If a person who still struggled to figure out the word order of "immigrant Asian wives" and "Asian immigrant wives" was able to raise a child in this country, our kids should be fine. Besides, he wasn't alone. He would have his girlfriend, me, and her parents. The child would be loved by so many people. And just as Alex had, the child would bring abundant joy to the parents.

When I freed myself from my own prejudice, I hit the greatest spiritual plateau. Yes, mental freedom was much more important than physical freedom. The lump I had been holding in my chest for a long time, which I used to torture myself, was finally melting away. I've got to start taking vitamins. I must live long for their baby.

On the following Saturday, my son told me he was going to his girl-friend's house at night.

"I'm thinking about your future and your baby. I think I'll be okay. I mean we'll be okay," I said as I followed him to his room.

"What?"

"I was afraid that having a baby would make you unhappy. But that was my fear, and I realized the same incident can make other people happy. So I won't worry anymore about you having sex with your girl-friend,"

"I told you, we watch movies in the living room and her parents will be in and out."

"Of course it's okay, if you wear a condom. I'm just telling you I'll be honored to be a grandmother."

"I won't have sex."

"Why? I said it's okay."

"Because I'm only fifteen and I want to go to college. I bet she does too."

"But you're a teenager. And by nature, they are impulsive, romantic, and unrealistic. You will have sex and when you do, there is a chance . . ."

"STOP!" he shouted in English. "Just leave me alone! I said I don't want to, okay. She doesn't want to either. Why do you keep bringing that up? All you think about is sex. You are disgusting. I just want to spend time with someone I care about!"

*Care*. Before a baby, before sex, and before love, there are two people who simply enjoy being with each other.

"Please, please, Mom, just leave me alone," he said. He was in the corner of his room, his head down and his arms in front like he was protecting himself. I'd seen him in that exact position at his karate dojo when he was scared of being hit. Did I do this?

"I'm so sorry, Alex."

"I don't know why you're so worried. I mean I know because you care about me, but you know I'm not stupid. I can think."

I had always been able to make him feel better, but I knew, this time, only our distance could heal him. I left the room.

The sad thing about being fifteen was that you had to be driven to your destination when no bus was available, and the biggest protest you could make in response was to sit in the backseat of your mother's car. Two hours later, Alex asked me to drop him off at his girlfriend's house. He sat in the back and we said nothing.

"Do you want to meet Abigail's parents? They are very nice," he said right before he got out.

"Yes, I do." *My future in-laws!* I wanted to joke, but I knew he probably hadn't recovered from our last talk.

I followed him to the front door. As soon as the door opened, Alex and Abigail disappeared inside.

"Oh, so good to see you again." The mother hugged me. "We love Alex! Abigail couldn't be happier since they started dating. Tonight, they're going to cook for us. I've bought all the ingredients for quiche. He is such a good boy. He is always welcome to stay at our house. He's like our son to us."

They insisted that I should come back for dinner. I declined their invitation politely and told them I'd be back at eleven. Abigail's mother said they understood. "No rush. Enjoy your free night," she said.

I went to my car and stayed a bit. I had no plans for the night. Their large living room window faced the street where I was parked, and behind the sheer curtain, I saw shadows crossing back and forth. The white curtain and the warm light that cast shadows. Alex was in the midst of mundane happiness, and I watched it from outside.

I arrived at five minutes after eleven. He got into the passenger seat.

"Did you have fun?" I asked.

"Yes," he replied.

"I'm glad," I said and started driving.

"You know, the baby talk you did earlier. Were you doing the reverse psychology thing?" he asked.

"No, I was not. I was serious. I had this enlightening experience at a sake bar and that led me to accept being a grandmother. My mind was free from pain, and I saw a bright future ahead of us."

"A sake bar; they must have served you some shit, Mom."

"They also serve fake sushi."

"What's that?"

"California rolls, Boston rolls, dragon rolls, rock-n-rolls, you know."

He laughed and said, "You know, I talk about you to Abigail all the time."

"Like what?"

"Like this. Things you do and say are so weird and my friends find it entertaining, especially when you're serious about it. All other parents are, how do you say, nice, right-minded, boring."

I laughed with him. I was already in his memories and soon would only be in his memories. He could find his own happiness, I thought. From now on, I'd find myself more of an observer than a participant.

"What if I told you that I decided to marry your father only after I found out that I was pregnant?"

"What? What's that got to do with me?"

"Well, everything, if the what-if was true, no? I'm only wondering because I saw a Japanese reality TV show the other day and—"

"Okay, Mom. First, you watch too many Japanese reality TV shows. You know they aren't really real. Second, I'm too busy living now to care about how I came to be. My life is happening as we speak. It's here and now. And it's all mine."

"Am I too narcissistic?"

"Nah, more like self-absorbed. People just don't care about you as much as you care about yourself."

"That is narcissistic."

He laughed.

"Besides, I'm five foot nine and know more English than you do. I'm a healthy ordinary person with a bit of a big ego and you still drive me to my girlfriend's house and pick me up at eleven P.M. Do you get my point?"

"My baby." I stroked his cheek.

He rested his face on my hand and cooed.

I told myself to remember this moment, his skin, his profile from the driver's seat, and the love that drove me to madness.

創発 (*souhatsu*):
emergence

# Eviction

AS I WAS PASSING THROUGH A SLEEPY NEIGHBORHOOD THIS MORNING after I walked my son to his elementary school, I thought, *Why am I still here?* The street was filled with the smell of seven-dollar-a-cup coffee and twenty-dollar plain omelets with a piece of watercress on top, both of which I did not dare spend money on, nor could I afford. San Francisco, the city for wealth and genius. I was hanging in here not because of my talent or effort, but solely by my luck. I wake up with a dream of being evicted and at night I pray with gratitude for having a roof over me. Abraham Maslow, the creator of the "hierarchy of needs," said that one must feel secure enough in food, shelter, clothing, and safety before being able to love someone. If Abraham Maslow saw me, he would say, "See this woman. This is a great example of a person who will never reach self-actualization."

*What if, after my husband's death, I decided to move back to Japan? What would be waiting for us?* The thought runs through my head as I enter the next neighborhood. The smell of money turns into the smell of urine and desperation. People wrapped in dusty blankets are sleeping in front of a shattered storefront. My son and I could be them tomorrow.

If I was living in Japan, the morning would start just like here. I would cook chopped daikon radish in a small pot. Next to the pot, I'd boil water for green tea and when the white daikons turned transparent, I'd turn off the heat and dissolve miso in the pot. By the time I'd wake my son up, there would be a bowl of rice and miso, a pot of green tea, and seasonal fruits.

My son would brush his teeth while I comb his hair. His curly hair hates a comb. The more I try, the bigger and puffier his hair gets. Eventually, I'd give up straightening his bird-nest head and take him to the school morning group.

On the way back, instead of the seven-dollar coffee and the organic omelet, I would smell the morning dew on the weeds. If it were spring, I'd be welcomed by the lazy warm air. If summer, I'd be feeling the impatient sun on my back. If fall, I'd breathe in deeply the delicious putrid smell of nuts under the yellow ginkgo trees. If winter, I'd be hopscotching on the frozen puddles. I might bump into some moms who don't know what to say to a single mother who returned from America. They would say "good morning" and smile at me as they drop their garbage on the curb. I would smile back to show that I am not their enemy.

We would probably be living in an apartment in front of my parents' condo. The brand-new four-unit apartment resembles a Victorian house. But instead of redwood, it's built with concrete, and the color of the house would be gray or beige, dull like a school uniform, to keep harmony with the surroundings, no bright colors, no pink, purple, or yellow. Five hundred dollars a month, the same price that some people charged renters to use closet space as a room in San Francisco. The window of my room faces my parents' condo. I could spy on my parents, but they could also spy on me.

I'd have a job at the nearby shopping mall, probably at a travel agency. Because I used to live in America, they say, therefore, I am an expert in America. All the places I've lived and loved, I'd turn the pages of my album to my customers and say, "The best part of these places are the people and the night sky. You wouldn't believe how kind people can be." I'd tell stories about the canyon in Casper, Wyoming, the cowboy bar in Greeley, Colorado, and the hippie drum circle in Salt Lake City, Utah. "We'd like to take a vacation to a major city where we don't have to speak much English and never need to worry about gun violence," they tell me. My customers are families and old couples who want to travel to the part of America where they can take photos for their holiday card and shop at an outlet mall. I push my pictures aside and pull out a brochure for a Honolulu vacation package.

At lunch break, my favorite time of the day, I buy two pastries at the shopping mall bakery. One is a shell-shaped roll with chocolate cream filling, and the other is a deep-fried donut filled with red bean paste. I pay three dollars in total and eat them at the back of the office with leftover green tea from breakfast in a thermo-bottle.

I work from Tuesday through Saturday (one-weekend-day attendance is mandatory for a customer service job) from 9:00 to 4:00. On Saturday, my son goes to my parents' condo so I can work until 10:00 P.M. It's seven dollars per hour. A minimum-wage job that I can do almost with my eyes closed. I don't describe my job with like or dislike but as stable.

I arrive home at 4:20 and within thirty minutes my son comes home. If it's spring, with warm wind; if it's summer, in a sweaty T-shirt; if it's fall, with a pocket full of acorns; and if it's winter, with a rosy-cheeked smile and crystallized snot under his nose. He'd burst into the door saying, "I'm hooooome!" He would wash his hands and find a Pokémon steamed bun on the table. He'd shove it all in his mouth and wash it down with milk. Less than five minutes later, he is out to the park by bicycle to meet with his friends.

While he is out, I vacuum the floor and run to a grocery store by bicycle. If it's spring, I'll cook cabbage roll with soft spring cabbage leaves; if it's summer, I'll make cold noodle garnished with cucumbers, steamed chicken, and canned mandarin orange on the top; if it's fall, I'll bake fatty mackerel pikes and ground radish on the side; and if it's winter, I'll set a clay pot over a portable stove in the center of our table and prepare tons of thin-sliced Wagyu beef, tofu, green onions, and other vegetables my son won't eat unless they're in the pot dish. I carry them back in a basket attached behind my bicycle, feeling the sunset behind me.

On the way home, I might bump into one or two of his classmates' moms. They ask if I will send Alex to a cram school once he starts middle school. I say, "Possibly." At the end of the conversation, they'll conclude, "I'm sure you're eventually going back to America. You don't have to go through what *we* have to go through." The six o'clock bell telling kids to go home rescues me from the moms. I leave them, saying I must start cooking dinner.

I fill hot water in a bathtub and when I begin to prepare for dinner, my son comes home. He sits at the dining table and winces in front of a massive amount of homework. The textbooks and his notes build a wall around him, and I cannot see his face to read his emotions. After his homework and a long soak in the deep bathtub, we eat dinner together. While we eat, I ask him what his friends from San Francisco might be doing right now. He shrugs, a common American gesture known among Japanese, and stuffs rice in his mouth. He tells me that his class is taking a field trip to the Houses of Parliament on Friday. They are allowed to spend five dollars for snacks, strictly five, he emphasizes. "I've already gone to the Shimazaki Candy store with Ken and spent exactly five dollars."

The only drinks that they're permitted to bring are water and tea.

If the teacher finds out that you brought juice, he will dump it out in front of the entire class. *Miseshime*—punishment by embarrassment, to oppress the other members in the community. There is no translation for the word in English and the closest thing I can think of is "public execution" during the colonial era of America.

"Fruit is not a snack," he continues, "so pack me tons of strawberries." He eats the last grain of rice stuck on the edge of the bowl and rinses his mouth with tea. My son uses chopsticks very well (unlike he does in reality).

After dinner, we watch a TV show together until 9:00 P.M. The show is called *The Amazing Globe*. It introduces inspiring stories from all over the world. My son is wowed by the American dad who completed a full marathon pushing his son in a wheelchair or by a cat that fought with a grizzly bear to protect the daughter of its owner.

"There are so many incredible stories out there, Mama!" my son, who has much lighter skin than I have, millions of freckles, and hazel eyes, tells me.

As I watch his face completely mesmerized by people from his birth land, I think: *What if at the time of my husband's death, I'd tried to hang on to San Francisco? What kind of life might we have?* I am haunted by the thought. *Life is to live not to maintain,* and as the quote runs in my head, my eyes get teary.

He brushes his teeth and goes to the bathroom. He slips into his futon. While I hear his sounds of sleep next to the living room, I count the money in my savings and calculate how much I can save for the next few years. I promise myself, even if I become penniless there, by the time he goes to high school we are moving back to the States—the place where the TV show happens in real life, the city I dreamed I would live in with my husband and my son.

# A Missing Toe

WE TAPED UP ITS SOFT FOOTPADS AND WATCHED THE CAT FRANTICALLY run under the house with its tail puffed up. The day started like a boring déjà vu, predictable and slow, a guaranteed lazy afternoon with the cat, our blind grandfather, and his favorite radio show, a Chinese language lesson. It was our usual way to kill time growing up as children when we visited my grandparents' house in the summer.

Now the cat exited off the stage, and my cousin, my little brother, and I sat in the sunroom, occasionally giggling and making faces in front of my grandfather. Because of my grandfather's long-retired eyes, the last of his senses he relied on were his ears, but as a result, he had lost most of his hearing too.

"Ask about his toe," my cousin, who lived with my grandparents, whispered.

"What happened to your toe?" I asked my grandfather.

"Daichi?" my grandfather asked, unsure who had spoken.

"No, it's his sister. WHAT HAPPENED TO YOUR TOE?" I spoke to him slowly.

"My toe?" He turned off the radio, then lifted his left foot and wiggled his toes like octopus's legs, the big toe missing.

"Ew!" my little brother and I screamed, with the same expression we'd made when my cousin brought a dead weasel down from the attic. My cousin laughed.

"You see that toe." My grandfather pointed to where the toe used to be, then continued, "Russians did it. They captured me in China while I worked as a translator, and after we lost the war, they sent me to a forest in Siberia to chop wood in the snow. They barely gave us food."

"So, he ate his toe." My cousin nudged me and stuck his tongue out.

I held my hands up to my mouth, my lunch welling up to my chest.

"I had frostbite and had to cut it off." My grandfather rubbed his foot. "We sat on the tree trunk and ate bark, Yoshino and I, clinging to each other to stay warm. I hate Russians." He gave a glimmer of a smile when he said "hate," looking up to the ceiling. His expression reminded me of a picture of a blind soul musician I had seen in an English textbook.

The sweat that built up behind my knees crawled down to my ankles as the cicadas' chorus began to insult my ears, but my toes continued to open and close, trying to warm up as I felt the harsh Siberian winter inside me. I glanced at my cousin and my little brother. They had moved on to singing rounds of the Frog Song, harmonizing in different keys in front of the fan. Their vibrating voices sounded like the speech of a robot.

"What did you do after Russia?" I asked my grandfather.

"I came back to Japan and married your grandmother. We met at the temple." He pointed his thumb right over his shoulder, in the direction of the temple where we always played hide-and-seek in the graveyard. "The monk arranged our meeting and that was it."

"That's all?" I said.

"Ice cream truck!" my grandmother shouted from the front door.

My cousin and my brother, who were now pushing each other to be in front of the fan, got up and dashed for the door.

"Yes, why?" my grandfather replied after a small delay.

"Would you have married if the monk had introduced you to a zombie?"

He laughed, and his glasses slid halfway down his nose.

"Did Russians take your sight away from you too?" I asked.

"No, that's hereditary, but don't worry, you don't have it. I married a stranger. Your mother also married a stranger," he said.

"What do you see now?" I asked.

"Imagine you are looking at frosted glass through a straw. That's what I see," he said.

I made a little circle with my thumbs and index fingers and looked through it. The straw vision emphasized my grandfather's missing toe even more.

"Come sit." He scooted to the side and patted the seat next to him, so we sat together in his round rattan chair. The cushion was flat and damp with the smell of fermented beans from my grandfather sitting on it all day. In the dressing mirror across the room, we looked like newlyweds, our backs straight for the first self-portrait, him in his red checkered shirt and me in my pink hibiscus dress.

I shimmied over to the edge of the chair to remove myself from the image in the mirror, but my grandfather wrapped his arm around my head and gently drew me closer. I let my head rest on his chest. With his other hand, he stroked my eyebrow. Then his fingers began to trace my eyelids, right ear, right cheek, traveled up to my forehead, and down my nose. Finally, his fingers reached my lips.

"You have grown so much since I last saw you," he told me with the same smile he gave when he said he hated Russians.

Click, the radio turned on and the familiar slow erhu melody, a touch of sweet melancholy, burst forth, followed by the five o'clock Chinese lesson. His hands left me to walk to the radio on the floor.

"Your ice cream is melting! Are you coming or not?" My grandmother called me from the front door.

"I have to go." I hopped away off the chair and ran.

"He met me, my grandpa," I told my grandmother. "He has met me before."

"Yes, I know. You didn't know? You're the first and the only grandchild he met."

"Me? Just me?"

"Yes, yes. Come, before your cousin eats your ice cream," she said.

I turned back by the front door. My grandfather was speaking Chinese to the radio, and I held my hands to my ears, slowly covering my eyes from the sides until I could frame him in my straw vision.

# Elegy for Mr. Aoki

"OF COURSE, SHE'LL PASS OUT BEFORE SHE CHOKES HERSELF TO death, but if Grandma begins to whine about living, you ask her about Mr. Aoki. You might find the story of Mr. Aoki to be quite entertaining," my mother said.

My mother was going to a buffet dinner at a hot springs hotel with Alex, leaving her mother to me. She told me that the place where her friend had made a reservation six months ago had been featured on the six o'clock news as one of the most exclusive restaurants, but with a child under age five, they could get a half-price deal.

Before the date, my mother took Alex to a department store to buy him a suit, in addition to her new summer dress. Apparently, this place was a huge deal among her grandma community—used for some sort of a grandchild unveiling.

"Can you taste anything in the place where a bunch of toddlers are crawling under the table?" I asked.

"The place is incredible. They have one-hour daycare attached to the buffet course. At half price and kid's meal. How could I pass up this opportunity?" she said.

"It sounds like a fancy version of Ikea to me," I said.

So I spent the day with my grandma. I spent, I said, but my grandma didn't wake up to join me for a cup of tea. She didn't move from her bed, period. I was impressed by how much she was able to sleep after she spent all night sleeping. "Sleep inversion," people called it when they slept during the day and were up all night, but in the case of my grandmother, day, night, tomorrow, and today all meant the same, so "sleep fusion" might be the better expression. Surely, if you spent most hours in your dreams, they would become your reality. *It's just a dream, glad it was a dream;* we were always looking down on our dreams. Why did we do that when both were part of our precious experience?

As the evening neared, the scent of moist asphalt came through the window. The Japanese summer squall—although I'd left this country many years ago, I could still tell by its smell. I took in the laundry, and when I brought the last futon mattress inside, the sky grew darker, and the first few drops splashed on the veranda. Just in time.

I was a daughter who had left my parents' home but hadn't yet been fully independent. The only repayment I could make to my mother was to hang and fold the laundry. My mother fed me and Alex for eight weeks while we visited Japan and took us to amusement parks and other places on weekends. Of course, my father worked for the money, but since I was little, I had always consulted about money with my mother and thanked only her. The way I understood it was that my mother was the front door, and my father was the pillar of our house. Once I broke into the front door, the rest was easy. He would not say no to my mother's request.

I observed my grandmother's face as I was folding the towels. My grandma had no chin. Her jawline sloped very gently, almost straight from her chin to her neck. Perhaps because of that, she snored when she slept. We used her snoring as a confirmation of her survival.

"Alex. Mission! Mission! Go check on Grandma and report me

back. Roger?" my mom would yell from the kitchen, and Alex would run to my grandma and stand on tiptoe by her bed to place his ear to her mouth.

And he'd yell back.

"Grandma alive, check, Roger!"

"Roger!" said Mom.

Alex then would come back, with fairylike, light footsteps, and snuggle next to me in the living room.

I loved seeing those two's, no, three's interactions. I had given Alex a snippet of the fun of being in a big family. The smell of delicious food prepared by someone other than his mother, the cheerful anime songs played on the TV, and the slightly depressed grandma in the next room—when I thought of this very ordinary image of a Japanese family, I thought I might have done something good, something decent as a mother.

Just as I was finishing folding all the towels, Grandma stopped snoring, and her arms agilely stretched up to the ceiling. *EEK!* I screamed a bit because she moved so quickly.

"Grandma, are you awake?"

"I'm always awake."

"Since this morning?"

"From the morning till night, I'm up waiting to die. I wish I could wait in my sleep, but I can't. I can't even go poop."

Her hand stretched to the ceiling repeated an open-and-close motion. She seemed to be grabbing something.

"Do you need something?"

"A tie."

"A tie?"

"Yes, to strangle myself."

*My goodness!* My heart skipped; then I came to my senses: I wasn't going to give her a tie, and if she wanted one, she'd find it in my father's closet right there, three steps away from her bed. My grandmother could walk. However, according to my mother, for the last six months, my grandmother got out of her bed voluntarily only to go to the bathroom and to the dining table on the night of the roasted eel dinner. So she should be okay. Still, I wouldn't be able to read a book in the next room in peace, seeing her hand bulging out from the top of her bed. Especially now that I knew what she desperately wanted.

Then, I remembered my mother's magic words.

"Grandma, tell me about Mr. Aoki."

Her face smoothed and turned peach color. Just as her face gained the color, her arms lowered down.

"Mr. Aoki was a wonderful man," my grandma said with a full smile.

"Who is Mr. Aoki?"

"He was a handsome soldier who came from Tokyo. He was sent to Kumamoto station during the war, and I was a typist there. He had dimples on his cheeks when he smiled. He had luxuriant hair and was a good man."

"Were you guys dating?"

"He often gave away his soldier ration to me and my family. We occasionally went out to eat, and he went back to Tokyo eventually."

"Was he your first love?"

"He was more like the only person I ever loved."

"How about my grandfather?"

"He was more like a person I was bound to by a common destiny. Kyoko, let me tell you something. I can control my dream. In my dream, I am invincible."

"Is that why you sleep all the time?"

"I told you. I am always up waiting to die. The snoring is my act put on for my daughter. I have been living for the last few years only to dream, but I'm tired now. The will is indelible, and no matter how much you try to abandon it, it overtakes your body. Even when I'm doing nothing, the will is working. That is even more true in my dream. Now the only thing that disobeys my will is my bowel movement. We can't deceive ourselves, can we?"

Suddenly, yes, once again suddenly, Grandma started speaking.

*This is for you and your family*
You gave me a can of the red beans and a soap bar,
supplies which only a soldier could receive.
You sneaked them into my sleeve.
You said you didn't like sweets.
Mr. Aoki, a bar of soap isn't sweets.
This was the only time I was thankful for the war.

*Doesn't it taste good?*
At the only cafe that was open,
I, a plain pan-fried noodle, and you, watered-down tea.
Through the crack of the window, the wind brought the scent
    of sea.
Inside, window fogged with our steam, and outside clouded black
    with soot.
While we'd never known when the next bombs would be dropped,
our inside remained peaceful.

*Come with me to Tokyo*
You wrapped my cold hand into your big warm hands.

Rumor said the war was ending.

Mr. Aoki, I was happy just to hear you sayin' that,

but just like you, I was an adopted and only child.

As I felt your heartbeat against my hand,

I looked down and shook my head.

*I will write to you* . . .

Half of what you said disappeared with the noise of the train.

Still with my forced smile, I nodded to everything.

You saluted me, and I bowed deeply,

never raising my face.

When I saw my tears dropped to the ground,

I knew the war was over.

"Grandma! Did you recite your love poem just now?"

"It's our little story."

"You're rappin', Grandma. Recite it again."

*This is for you and your family* . . .

My grandma started.

"Again."

*This is for you and your family* . . .

This time, she did it with a little more intonation, as if she was singing a traditional-style Japanese song.

*I must record this!* I ran to look for a camera.

"Grandma, wait a minute. Don't let your dream take you away."

When I returned to her, Grandma was snoring.

"Snoring is an act done for your daughter. Grandma, come on, sing the song of Mr. Aoki."

I hit record on the camera.

Grandma opened one eye and looked at me. The edge of her mouth faintly curved to smile.

"Will is a hassle. Will is a trouble," she said and sighed.

Grandma's bony hands begin to beat time on her chest.

*This is for you and your family* . . .

I studied the camera and focused on Grandma's face.

I joined the chorus lip-syncing so that the camera wouldn't capture my voice and watched my grandma sing through the screen.

# The Bone Gatherers

FOR THE DAY OF MY GRANDMOTHER'S ONE-YEAR MEMORIAL, MY SON and I came back to Japan. On the train to the cemetery, my father stared at a paperback detective novel with a sullen look. Normally, he would be flipping pages one after another, pulling his nose hair or picking at his ear. Today he had been staring at the same page since we got on the train, while the view behind his window passed like a movie set to fast-forward.

I was sitting across from my father with my mother and my brother. My son sat on my brother's lap, playing Rock, Paper, Scissors, with the winner pinching the other's cheek. My brother's cheek was turning bright red. Though the game is solely based on luck, my brother knew how to lose. It had been an hour at least since they started playing. Every chance my son could get, he held my brother's hand, leg, or anywhere he could hold. My brother was good with a small child. He had never been married, no girlfriend either, maybe never.

"Your father still has not spoken to Tetsuo," my mother whispered into my ear.

Tetsuo used to be my father's brother. I say "used to be" because a few years ago my father declared to my mother that he'd cut off all family ties with Tetsuo. For one simple reason: My father was against giving prolonged life support to my grandmother, but despite his opposition, Tetsuo, my uncle, my grandmother's medical executor, my father's only sibling, had asked the doctor to make a hole into my grandmother's belly in order to give her nutrition.

"The mummy at Ueno Museum looked healthier than your grandmother," I remember my mother telling me over the phone. My grandmother survived for another two years until Tetsuo decided to take the tube out of her stomach. She would still be alive if my uncle hadn't let her go; her dried-bean-sprout body quietly occupying the corner of the hospital room.

"Your uncle's always been too soft, can't let go of things. He was like that too when his father died," my mother said as the train approached our destination.

As I was growing up, whenever we visited my father's grandparents' house on the weekend, we would always find my uncle at home. My little brother and I climbed up their narrow staircase on hands and knees, trying not to scrape our arms on the sandpaper-textured wall. We always found Tetsuo, who resembled a depressed bear, reading a magazine in the middle of his unlit room. His thick black hair was cut like freshly mowed grass. He was tan, always tan. He must have had white eyes, but his eyeballs disappeared under his fat eyelids, barely showing two black pupils. We slowly clawed toward him, still on four legs, then "Wa!" We jumped onto his neck. Tetsuo murmured with a sticky summer air voice, "You guys again?" He didn't hug us back or push us away either, just retreated to his magazine. He never gave us toys in fine crisp paper bags. He instead gave us several Hershey bars and a bunch of Japanese sparklers. "I won those at the slot machine," he would say with the same damp voice. "Don't eat them all at once. They're from America, twice as sweet as ours."

In the corner of his room, the magazines piled up. On the front cover of one, a man was posing—showing off his washboard abs and smiling with teeth so white that it appeared they would glow in the dark. Next to the magazines, several dumbbells lay on the tatami floor, so heavy that when we tried to pick them up to imitate the models in the magazines, we could see deep impressions, the color of fresh green tatami. Once we were bored with posing like those men, we began to push Tetsuo with our backs against his back. Tetsuo didn't budge so we pushed him some more. Then he purposely fell forward. We repeated the push-and-fall dance, and eventually he growled, saying, "All right, let's go for a walk." Wearing his familiar worker's uniform over his white T-shirt, he slipped into his geta clogs and took us outside. To most of our questions, he responded either "Hmmm" or "Hah." Hearing his clogs going clip-clop, we tried to catch up with him. His work uniform changed color in the sunlight. It looked faded green or sometimes gray. It was such a wispy color, but nothing more perfectly suited his bulky body.

I still remember the one day he abandoned his worker's uniform, the only time I had ever seen him without it. It was the day of my grandfather's funeral. I was nine years old.

I can recall a glimpse of my grandfather's white bones at the funeral home contrasting with my uncle's black suit. The bones had just come out from the crematory, and when I inhaled, the heat rose to my eyes. The tabletop stood just above my chin. I was the closest to the burnt remains of my grandfather. I inhaled again, slowly, to see if I could smell death, but all I could smell was the scent of mothballs coming from my great-aunt who was standing next to me.

On the table, my grandfather's shattered bones were spread, reminding me of the fossil puzzle from the summer festival. I was disappointed that I could not see his complete skeleton. "Just one piece," my mother said as she handed me a long pair of chopsticks. My mother and I picked a piece of my grandfather which looked like dead coral that had washed ashore. We dropped it into a small clay pot, then passed the chopsticks to my aunt. Again, facing my grandfather, I followed the bones as they were picked and dropped into the pot. The chopsticks and the pot were passed to each family member, and as my father chose the last bone, the mortician arrived and rolled the table containing all that was left of my grandfather to another room.

I asked my mother if a dead body is *really* cold.

"You could have touched him," my mother said in the cab as we were leaving the crematorium. What I was excited about most that day was wearing my brand-new black pleated skirt, skipping school, and spending the night at my grandparents' house. What I regretted was seeing my grandfather off without touching his body, so I could tell my friends that a dead body is really cold.

With a tie and a fedora, even on the weekend; his posture upright as if a ruler had been implanted in his back; and his angry Noh-mask-like facial expression, my grandfather had always seemed distant. His death felt to me no more painful than plucking a single hair from my head.

That night, after the bone-gathering ceremony, the pot of my grandfather's bones was placed on the Buddhist altar in my grandparents' living room. My father and the other male relatives, after drinking sake, lay about like slumbering sea lions on a pier in front of my grandfather. Other than my grandmother, who had gone to bed right after the ceremony, all the women were cleaning the kitchen, talking excitedly about Auntie Sachiko's second husband, who was ten years younger than she was and looked just like an actor in a toothpaste commercial. As I passed them to go upstairs, I glanced in the living room once again and saw the big funeral picture of my grandfather. He was staring at me and looked even scarier than I remembered. Trying to avoid eye contact, I carefully stepped between my father and the other relatives. But I couldn't escape my grandfather's gaze. Suddenly, I realized that he now could appear as a ghost to curse us, the men, who were passed out beneath him; the women, whose only interest was in family gossip; and me, who wanted to touch his body to prove to my friends that a dead body is cold. I put my palms together, praying and apologizing to my grandfather for our lack of respect.

"You can't sleep either?" Tetsuo, still wearing his black suit, was standing behind me.

My uncle didn't drink so he had been hiding in his room while everyone had gotten drunk in the living room. His thick eyelids were puffier than ever, but I could see bloodshot lines in the whites of his eyes.

Maybe because he was wearing black or because I had never seen him in a suit, his shoulders seemed narrower than usual. He didn't look like a bear, he instead looked like a stink bug that could fall over with one flick of a finger and never get up.

I pointed to my grandfather's picture, my face still down.

"Ah, he received it when he returned from the war," my uncle said.

I didn't understand what he was talking about, but as I raised my head, I noticed a framed award hanging next to his picture.

"Why?" I asked.

"Because he hid behind a huge rock and didn't kill anybody."

I shook my head, looked at my uncle, and laughed without making a sound.

"It's true," my uncle said, "he killed nobody."

My uncle mussed my hair, then embraced me tightly.

From the train station, we took a cab to my grandparents' cemetery. My father sat in the passenger seat, still silent. My mother, my brother, and I squeezed into the backseat, and my son sat on my brother's lap. As we neared the cemetery, I looked out the window, hoping to spot my uncle before anyone noticed.

We reached my grandparents' grave and there was still no sight of Tetsuo. I asked my mother where he was and she whispered. "He is right there next to Uncle Toru."

Tetsuo was skinny, his thick black hair now white.

"He is a vegetarian now," my mother added.

The prayer lasted for twenty minutes; after that my father exchanged greetings with his relatives. My son and my brother held hands and headed to the ice cream vending machine at the management office. I stayed behind my father with my mother and bowed to my estranged relatives. As I rose from each bow, Tetsuo appeared in my sight in a different position in front of my grandparents' grave like in a slideshow; rearranging flowers in the vase, pulling tiny weeds, watering the gravestone, and wiping the water from it with his sleeve. His back no longer reminded me of a bear or a stink bug. He was now just a man in an oversized black suit. My father and my mother began to walk to the office, where my brother and my son waited for us. I followed my parents for one block until I told them I forgot my sun umbrella by the bench. I walked back to my grandparents' grave surrounded by the cicadas' chorus. From behind my uncle's back, I said, "Uncle Tetsuo?"

The last time I saw Tetsuo, I was twelve. I was awkwardly tall and slim. Although my breasts weren't developed yet, I had graduated from a flower-print undershirt to a sports bra and I was allowed to take the train to my grandmother's house by myself.

We went for a stroll after dinner. My uncle's geta clogs were clip-clopping still, his hand on the back of my neck, holding me like I was his kitten. I was tall enough to walk beside him and didn't have to catch up with him anymore. I don't remember what I was talking about, probably nothing. Tetsuo, as usual, was responding "Hmmm," or "Hah."

In between my chat and his nonchalant responses, I realized for the first time how little I knew about him. Why did he still live with my grandmother? Why wasn't he married? What did he do on the weekends when I wasn't there? Did he go out with a girlfriend, friends, or someone? I gazed up and saw his stubble beard growing on his chin and below his chin his big Adam's apple. We stopped at the traffic light. He noticed me looking up at him so he looked away. I felt his hand on my neck, his big warm hand—a man's hand, a man's heat. I wiggled and twitched slightly to move away from his hand but subtly, so subtly that only my heart would notice. But he felt it. I knew that he noticed because his eyes looked so sad, like the night he held me tightly in front of my grandfather's war award. And I believe I looked sad too, or perhaps scared, not of him but of the change I was about to go through. He moved his hand from my neck to point out the building in front of us and said, "See that tall building? That used to be the tannery where your grandfather worked. They used to make the finest briefcases. Your school bag—your grandfather made that too, cut the leather, sewed it together, all by himself."

The story contained no surprises. I'd heard it before from my father, but I gave Tetsuo an exaggerated nod. I didn't care what he said. All I wanted was for the traffic light to change so we could move forward or go back to the time before I was aware of our existence; him, his presence, and mine.

"Everything is changing in this neighborhood," Tetsuo said.

The traffic light turned green. His hand stayed by his side as we walked a little apart from each other.

# )|| "River"

ALEX COMES TO MY BED. HE COMES AS HE PLEASES. SOMETIMES FOR weeks in row and other times not for weeks. I lie next to him, his back against me. I wiggle my feet between his and rub his insteps, trying to remove any cold spots. His shins are hairy, but his feet are still smooth; then I recall he used to be a part of me.

"Scratch my back," he tells me, so I insert my hand under his shirt. He purrs.

My thighs to his thighs, my kneecaps to the concave of the backs of his knees, we're about the same height.

"To the left, below my shoulder blade," he says and pushes his back to me.

"I am as far left as I can go. You have so much space on your side. Can you just move, and why do we need to share one pillow?"

He laughs but gives no sign of moving to his right. I push him back. "Stop." He gets grouchy and reluctantly accepts the second pillow.

"Feel my love. According to Bubbe, that pillow is the best on the market," I tell him, and he replies that he likes mine better. "You're sixteen and you still come to my bed," I say, still scratching his back.

"You're welcome," he says. "I'm leaving for Belgium in two years. So enjoy it while it lasts."

We settle into a comfortable position.

I always sleep on one half of the bed. It's a habit I developed when he was a baby. I slept on the left, Levi slept on the right, and bundled-up Alex slept in the middle. We slept like the kanji "river." Three lines, shortest line in the middle, longest to the right, and the left line in between the lengths of the other two; we called it a symbol of happiness.

I can now sleep in the center, spread out in the kanji "big." So much space I can take over without apology. But if the edge of my bed already satisfies me, what is the point of hoarding more? More land, more money, more material, more energy, more status, more, more, more, more. This isn't going to be part of my American dream, and no matter how American I become I'll fight against it.

Two lines of almost identical length with the tips of the lines entwined. Our world has not been discovered by anyone yet. I know no kanji that resembles us. What am I when my son is in my bed? We can't even be described in the three-thousand-year history, so leave us alone and let me enjoy his feet.

It's very hard to leave a warmed-up bed, but my day has just begun. One, two, three, and four . . . maybe five and six, then I jump up. Alex is snoring.

I warm the cast-iron pan on the stovetop, crack three eggs in a bowl, add some milk, whisk, and pour the mixture into the pan. I toss two waffles from Charlie's Cafe into the toaster. Five-dollar premade waffles; we indulge in this luxury on occasional weekends. I press the On button on the electric kettle, prepare two cups, and place a coffee dripper with filter on top of my cup. For Alex, I make green tea in a Japanese teapot. I cut one kiwi in half, *the superfood with more vitamin C than strawberries,* Alex has told me. I pour hot water slowly into the dripper, watching the coffee grounds rise and slowly sink. When the aroma of coffee spreads in the kitchen, I think this is how I wish to live my life every day. Eggs are ready, so are the waffles. Golden brown, yellow, and green, nicely arranged on two white plates.

Has anything changed in my life since he was three? We've lived in the same house and hung out with the same friends. I've kept the same job at preschool and Alex has kept growing and growing.

"Josh envies me," Alex tells me, biting into his waffle.

"Josh? The boy who can get straight A's without studying, whose parents are both from Stanford or Harvard or whatever big-name college? He can probably go to school as a legacy. Why?"

"Because he doesn't know what he wants to do with his life. I know exactly where I want to be and what I want to be. Not knowing what's ahead of you is like walking into a dark mystic river. You don't understand, do you? Knowing what we want to do with our lives is hard. I guess I'm ahead of everyone."

I smile and say, "Good. America isn't the only country on this earth. Everyone should be a minority once in their life. That's the only way we can understand what it feels like to struggle to communicate with others, face cultural clashes, and feel crippled and inferior; so you focus on listening to people rather than talking, to understand yourself and others. Listening is the key, but majorities never appreciate this. This is how we can develop compassion and a sense of identity, and—"

"Okay, okay, Mom," he says, holding his palm up to me, laughing. "Are you telling *me*?"

I laugh too.

"I can never be a majority, here, in Japan, or anywhere," he says.

*And don't ever try to be,* I want to say but I hold back my words. That is something for him to discover.

"Mmm, the tea is good. This is called luxury," he says.

"You've grown up to be a good boy."

"What is that supposed to mean?"

"Nothing. I just thought about it."

He shrugs, then starts to talk about the anime we watched last night. The movie was an hour and a half long, but people share their two-hour analysis videos and none of their opinions match. There is a depth to the story which no one has figured out, he tells me.

"So, what are you going to do after I leave?" he asks.

"Stay alive."

"How boring can you be?"

"Ha, boring. I've already done the most exciting and selfish thing humans can do."

"What's that?"

"To have a child."

The love that cannot be refused, the more you pour in, the more he absorbs, the life in which I can love one person as much as I want.

"What about your writing? Don't lie to me. It wasn't just a hobby or to get a good job like you told me. I know you. You hate spending money for yourself. But you did, to go to that school. Soon, you won't have to support me anymore. You know that I can build my life just fine without you. You can go broke all you want."

*What a wonderful life I have*, I think, and hold my breath. This has been my silly habit since I was a child, I hold my breath when I want to stop time.

While he is here with me, and after he leaves, I want to be here. I want to live.

# The Waves I Lust

*A BLACK CAT STOPPED IN THE MIDDLE OF THE ROAD AND LOOKED AT HER. Its eyes shone green. It was almost midnight; she was waiting for a bus. Her husband in America hadn't been answering her call. A presentiment that something bad would happen had been upsetting her—it made her sick to her stomach. When she saw the black cat, the presentiment turned into a conviction. Still, she got on the bus. Did she deny the feeling because she wanted to visit her best friend or did she deny it because she was afraid of falling apart at the bus stop? She couldn't remember. Perhaps the black cat was a story she made up. At least, this was how she always concluded.*

Do you know why I like you?

Because I read my story to you?

No, because it's two in the morning and you are still on the phone with me without judging what I do.

Do you know why I like you?

Because I listen to your story?

No, because you love your wife. I get to learn what it is like being miserable next to a loved one, without having to deal with the actual domestic pity.

I bet you loved your husband.

No, I trusted him and depended on him.

No, you loved him. That's why you hate me.

If I hated you, I wouldn't let you touch me. I am trusting you enough not to bite me off. Tell me how you're going to touch me.

*First, I'm kissing your forehead, then cheeks, ear, now both ears . . .* Masaoka quietly began through the phone. He unbuttoned my blouse, slowly and carefully, as if each button was a precious part of my body. Removing my blouse from my shoulders, he released one sigh and embraced me softly before he unhooked my bra. He ran his fingers down my back as his lips rested on my clavicle. He gently pushed me to the bed. Down and down, he descended. With each kiss, his warm breath and tongue tickled me, enough for me to beg. *Please, make your way.*

Even with such cheap descriptions, I could satisfy myself when I closed my eyes. My imagination was powerful enough to overcome Masaoka's clumsy scenario. I sighed deeply, loud enough for him to feel it over the phone. I made sure he reciprocated my sigh before I inserted my hand under my T-shirt. My fingers, still cold, flirted with my nipples, then I massaged my breasts. Down and down, I descended. While my body became wrapped in goosebumps, my fingers steadily absorbed the heat. By the time they reached between my legs, the temperature of my body and that of my fingers became one, drawing in my pool. My body, my fingers; his fingers, his tongue—all would lose their boundaries. His fantasy, my reality; his script, my imagination— all would lose their meaning.

Masaoka's voice was always muffled through the phone. His wife slept in the bedroom next to his. He spoke to me under the covers, almost whispering.

But I would not mix my reality and fantasy. I'd only answer his calls when my son was away.

———

*Why did you start surfing?*

This was his first question to me. We met for the first time on the side of a street while I was changing into my wetsuit.

Good morning, he said in English.

He was tall and had beautiful wavy hair, atypical for a Japanese man, but I could hear the faint familiarity in his greeting, so I asked if he was Japanese, and he said yes.

I've been surfing in the Bay Area for decades. But never met a Japanese girl.

I'm not really a girl. I'm in my thirties. I already have a child.

Well, you look like a girl to me.

The familiarity of the language brought us closer quickly. After we finished changing into our wetsuits, we began walking to the beach together.

I started surfing three months ago. But I have never caught a single wave. I've been basically coming here to get beaten by the ocean. I can't get past the breaking waves, I said.

You started surfing in winter, in the Bay Area, alone? You've got some guts. He smiled. The waves are small today. I'm just here to chill. Come with me. I'll take you to the lineup.

He stared at the ocean for a few minutes, then walked in until the water came to his chest. Suddenly, the ocean calmed down. *Waves are going back, hop on your board now and go!* I jumped on my board and followed him. The waves crashed on both sides of us but never in front of us. *They are avoiding Masaoka. Japanese Moses, he knows how to control the ocean.* Later when I told him about this thought, he laughed and said that he just aimed for the water that was going out. The current could take us to the lineup without much paddling. This way you wouldn't have to waste your energy and could conserve it for surfing. All waves eventually had to go back out, he told me. The first lesson: You learn to read the ocean.

Within five minutes, I arrived at the lineup, where other surfers waited for the next set. A few surfers waved at Masaoka, and he returned their greeting by lifting his chin up. When I was paddling so hard not to lose Masaoka, the ocean had appeared mean and evil. But out here, it transformed into a peaceful goddess. The sound of the splash that I made while I waited for the waves soothed my ears. *I'm alive,* I thought.

Lesson Two: Let everyone take the first wave of the set. This was the key, he said, for rookies like me and old men like him to catch waves without fail. *Now go,* he'd say, and I'd started paddling. Still, I couldn't catch a single wave while Masaoka caught a wave in every set. Each time he paddled back to the lineup, he waved at me. His long, messy hair covered his face and he pushed it back with a big smile. I saw that his wet skin shone under the spring sunlight. Like other surfers, he was tanned so evenly, but unlike others, he had no fishnet wrinkles, except smile lines. *I wonder what it would be like to trace those lines.* I remember thinking.

Why did you start surfing? he asked while we waited for the next set of waves.

I wanted to feel free.

Ah, everyone says that.

If I could bear being close to death, I'd have nothing to be afraid of. Then, I'll be free.

You're interesting. People feel free because they can control the wave even just for three minutes. Like they conquered mother nature. Besides, surfing has this power to cancel out all the bad things that have happened in your life. One wave and poof, all day you feel like nothing is a big deal.

I'm not interested in feeling good. I just need some confirmation, I said.

We started calling each other in the morning, checking on which beach was breaking, and met up to surf at least once a week. He was an acupuncturist and had his own practice. I was a mother of a small boy and about to be a student at a graduate school. For a week when the waves were breaking perfectly, Masaoka didn't take any patients during the day, only at night.

I live here because of the waves. Until a few years ago, I surfed at Mavericks in the winter. You don't have to compete. Anyone can surf there. The ocean belongs to everyone, Masaoka said.

Your wife doesn't come surfing with you? I asked.

She is not interested in what I do. Not interested in me anymore.

One morning, he called to tell me the waves would be breaking at a beach I had never heard of before. We would need to hike down a bit to get to the spot, but because it was hidden, and there would be no one surfing around us, it would be a perfect place for me to improve my skills.

Don't worry, Kyoko. You'll be safe with me. A bonus, it's got a public shower room with hot water.

He was right. In the deserted ocean, I didn't have to wait for my turn. I was able to try without worrying about other surfers, and when I missed the timing, I turned back to the lineup quickly and tried again. A small mountain of water, the color deeper than the sky, appeared far away. *Not yet. Wait until the fear of being swallowed by it rushing into me.* That was how I learned the timing to start paddling. The small friendly wave that I spotted far away became a big brutal force that wanted to destroy me. Five seconds after I felt like running away was the exact moment I needed to start to paddle.

If I missed the timing to catch it, either the wave passed me quietly or it grabbed me. When the wave tossed me around, I let it be until eventually my head popped out of the water. If I didn't panic, I could always come up. This was Masaoka's lesson three. *Cover your head under the water and protect yourself from your own surfboard. If you don't get a concussion, you'll survive and eventually resurface.*

By the end of the two-hour session, I no longer needed him to spot the sets for me. Masaoka was right. I was able to catch a bunch of waves.

After we were done, I was wrapped in a comfortable feebleness. Ocean water always made me feel sexy.

He took me to the public shower room, a handful of quarters in his hand.

See, I told you. No one comes here, Masaoka said.

We stood in front of the shower room, waiting for one of us to say something.

*He wants to go in with me.* I could sense the male energy from him, so I said, Would you like to go in with me?

He looked at me and nodded. For a moment, he turned into a high school boy who had been asked by a girl on a first date. He took my hand and led me into the dark room.

Under the warm water, we stripped each other's wetsuits off and kissed.

Come close to me. You'll be cold, he said.

He dropped quarters into the slot over and over, wanting not to run out of the warm water coming through the sprinklers. He held my shoulders, turned me around, and made me stand right under the showerhead. Although I knew there was something more he wanted and that might be the reason for his kindness, I couldn't help but be allured by his gesture. When was the last time a man had handled me so gently? We kissed and washed our kisses away under the water.

By the time we were both fully naked, I saw his body responding to mine. I stopped kissing and stood there, my hands on his shoulders, arms stretched out and my eyes looking down. The shower had stopped and the sound of water running down the drain was amplified.

Look what you've done to me. You've got to take care of me now, he said with a faint smile.

I placed my hand on his inner thigh. He leaned forward and rested his head on my shoulder. I slid my hand to his lower stomach. From here, there would be only one direction the hand should go next. He was waiting.

I pushed his chest away gently.

No, I'm sorry. I can't, I said. I don't want to touch you or see you naked below your waist.

He turned his back, and I wrapped my arms around him from behind while he rubbed himself. Pressing the soft part of my body to him, I kissed his back until he reached his orgasm.

Later in the parking lot, I made myself clear to him that he could touch me all he wanted but I would never reciprocate his need.

I promised myself, I said. I'll never do anything I don't want to do for men. *Never again.*

I see. I'm sorry about earlier. I really am and I apologize for what I've said to you. I also have something to tell you. The only woman I love is my wife. I'll never divorce her. I'll be aroused by your body and always desire you, but only because you fill my loneliness.

In that moment, I knew I could trust him.

*A few weeks before she was leaving to visit her parents in Japan, her husband was washing his classic car in his driveway. She was about to go for a walk with her son in a stroller.*

*"Enough of this guilt trip!" he said.*

*At the time, he had been asked by his mother in Boston to come home for the Jewish New Year.*

*It was the last year he was still alive.*

*"She says, come see my brother. He will be going to Iraq soon. They say after you guys leave to visit Japan, I'll be alone doing nothing anyway. They don't think I have a life here."*

*She listened to him complain while she pushed the stroller back and forth to put her son to sleep. The stories he told about his family always fascinated her. The more he was involved in the story the more he became animated, and the stories took unexpected turns. She forgot her initial plan to walk to the park and got lost in his talk.*

*"You should say no. It's not like someone is going to die if you say no," she said.*

*"Thank you! You understand me. I'm going to do that!" His face brightened.*

*His simplicity makes him look so cute, she thought. How could she explain to him that this was the best compliment she could give him? He was aiming for a strong, reliable father figure. So she kept the compliment to herself. Countless stories must be sleeping inside him, enough to entertain her for the rest of her life. And she had earned the privilege to elicit them. The husband continued chatting, hopping from topic to* topic—*the Impala that needed an overhaul, the five thousand dollars he lent to a punk boy across the street who had not returned from jail, and the marriage and childbirth of their former garage band member.*

*"I have been wondering for a long time. Why don't you write songs anymore? You used to write even during our house parties, locking yourself in the bedroom. We met through music. I can still recall the day I saw you at the BART station. You were wearing a plain white T-shirt and jeans, your guitar bag on your shoulder. You were so beautiful."*

*She thought about how to answer his question. She had forgotten about guitar, writing lyrics in broken English, and that they had met through his garage band. To recall the passion—as tangible as fog—that led her to be creative was beyond her capacity since all of these interests had become irrelevant to her life now . . . What had driven her to write in the past?*

*"I think there was something unsatisfactory in my life. I wanted to be heard so I wrote in my childish English, sang it out of tune with my awful guitar. But all lost meaning when I met you and our son. You guys will know me and that seems enough. I'm too content to write."*

*Her husband smiled big.*

*This was the last serious conversation she had with him that she could remember.*

When I finished reading, I lifted my face.

Mediocre. Sentimental. Pretentious. I could vomit now, I said.

The ocean was flat this morning. We finished the session in thirty minutes and drove to a café across from the parking lot. I brought a notebook that I always kept in the glove compartment and read a passage from it to Masaoka.

*But it was real.* The clothes Levi was wearing that day, the song I heard from the car radio, and the warm air that Indian summer had brought—I could remember all so vividly. It was real. It happened to me.

But soon, this would all be disguised as fiction and weaved into a bigger story. Joy, sorrow, laughter, tears, they would survive in bits and pieces to bedeck my story.

Have I ever told you that I was married before my wife? I even have a child, Masaoka said.

Never. Where is the child?

In Japan with her mother. My daughter was two when I saw her last at the airport. She will be twenty this year. My ex was from a wealthy family, and I was just the son of a baker. Do you like chestnuts? My parents' shop was highly renowned in Kyoto for Mont Blanc. I'll make you some in the fall when I pick chestnuts from my backyard. Anyway, after my wife graduated from two-year college, we eloped to America.

A quite typical story. I've heard similar stories from several other Japanese people before, I said.

We were so broke and so happy. We ate pasta with butter and soy sauce. We went to a free meal at a church, holding each other's hands. A year later, she got pregnant. I couldn't give up my dream to be a pâtissier in San Francisco. But she couldn't wait. We asked her parents if she and our daughter could live with them. Her parents welcomed the idea. They were no longer upset about our past once they knew they had a grandchild. I promised that I'd come get them when I was financially stable enough to support them. I went to school and worked at an Italian bakery in North Beach, but I realized I couldn't get a visa as a pâtissier. So I switched schools, got an acupuncturist license, worked day and night, and saved up money. Then I flew to Kyoto with a suitcase full of Ghirardelli chocolate. When I arrived at the door, it was her parents who answered. They said that I'd been living selfishly, and I was too cruel to come get my child and their daughter after five years. My daughter loved her school and finally had come to terms with a life without a father. Now I came to pull them away from the life they'd built, reexposing the wound. If I really loved my family, they said, I should leave now without seeing them. I had to agree. I chose life in America and the ocean. Who would want that kind of father?

So you haven't seen your daughter since she left America?

It wasn't easy like today. The best we could do was to make expensive phone calls. But the little kid's attention span is so short. Two minutes at best. Soon my ex-wife stopped answering my phone calls too.

It's a sad story. But you must know a father isn't as important as people think. Children can grow up completely fine without a father as long as the mother and child have money. Your story isn't as big a deal as you think. Don't worry. You're as ordinary as the old man who is picking up his dog's poop in front of us or the middle-aged man who is shoving his ham-and-cheese croissant into his mouth at the next table. A completely boring ordinary person who lives a completely boring life while having a completely boring past.

You loved your husband.

Again about my husband?

You are like the ball of a pendulum. You've been thrown in full force so rapidly that you are now scared to swing back in the opposite direction. So you wrap your legs around the pole, never to be swung again.

I laughed and said, you'd be a better romance novelist than I. The reality wasn't that glamorous. It wasn't a passionate love. He was more like a friend. After we had a child, it got worse. *I didn't even let him make love with me,* I thought but didn't say to Masaoka.

Then it was beyond love for you. You bare your teeth when a man becomes a relationship candidate. You only say yes to those who won't break you. So "friend" is the highest compliment you could give to men because it means you want to be with them without a time limit.

*That wasn't quite right.* I was only putting myself first. Even after you devoted countless time, exhausting your energy to please men, their last and only place was to sleep. Their lassitude and offhand attitude after they'd reached orgasm disgusted me. After they'd go, the loneliness accompanied me as if I was the only one left on Earth.

The orgasm and death might be the same thing. No matter how much you'd spent your time building something together, you had to reach the last destination alone.

The first time when I touched you, Masaoka said, I knew you had not been touched by anyone. I bet you had no one to carry your groceries for ages. You always look so cheerful in the ocean even after you're swallowed by a big wave. Blowing snot out your nose and following me like a stray puppy, I can't say you're pretty even just as flattery. But as soon as I touched your bare shoulders in the shower room, your muscles stiffened. *How could I leave her alone?* I thought. To be honest, I didn't want to know that side of you because then . . . it would be too much for me or for you. I wouldn't be able to think of you as just another surf girl. But my fingers, they can sense even if I refuse to know. A sad fate of being a *genius* acupuncturist.

He deliberately brushed his wavy hair back and smirked. His kindness—his best effort to lighten up the atmosphere.

I stopped blinking so as to keep my tears from spilling out of my eyes. I shifted my focus to the man who was eating the ham-and-cheese croissant. I regretted belittling him earlier to belittle Masaoka. This man had his own drama and tragedy that he had to face and had to overcome before he arrived at this café. It wasn't only me who was trying to survive.

It's your turn. Let's talk about your wife. What does she do?

A soul searcher.

What? What is that?

She goes to a retreat in Santa Fe, stays on a mountain somewhere in Peru for a week without communication, and one fourth of the year she spends in our Kauai island house with her female friends, chasing her guru. She and her friends cook for him and his students or his lovers, who knows what! She completely ignores me. She has become a typical Japanese middle-aged woman.

A middle-aged Japanese woman is my idol! People who have surpassed gender frameworks! Did you know in South Korea, they call these women ajumma? If I met your wife before I met you, I'd for sure ignore you and be friends with her. Too bad that that didn't happen.

Oh, give me a break.

We laughed together. It was between morning and noon. A peaceful and ambivalent time where only people who did not have to do anything and who did nothing would be out.

Do you want to be with an American man again?

No American, no Japanese, no men, period.

Too bad. You're wasting your youth. Really too bad. If I were you, I'd be dating a different man every week. Wait, that's impossible for you because no man meets the requirements you demand of them except me. I have *intimate* knowledge of what you want and how you want it.

*Idiot.* All men, no matter where they were from, possessed the same attitude. They believed they could make the entire population of women fall in love with them if they tried hard enough.

But what filled my mind at the time was *Mont Blanc*, the dessert I had never seen at an American bakery. When was the last time I had eaten it? Chestnuts in fall. He had promised me something sweet which I would have to wait for for another few months. That gave me a flutter in my chest.

To see Masaoka in clothes besides training outfits made me a little uneasy. It reminded me that he existed outside the ocean. In a polo shirt and chinos, he looked a bit older than he did when he wore a wetsuit or sweatshirt. A few gray hairs here and there and the creases around his eyes were permanently engraved. These signs of aging comforted me. He was just like everyone. Under the big sky and in the ocean, he was a reliable teacher who could rescue me from danger. In the closed room, he was still a bit of a stranger, which made our meeting all the more thrilling.

I'd always visited him in a white blouse and jeans with minimal yet impeccable makeup. I checked out my hair in the car's rearview mirror and applied mint-scented lip balm. I would rather die than have Masaoka find out I made these tiny efforts before our meetings.

I didn't use the garage attached to his office building. I always parked on the street a few blocks away, where there were no parking meters, and walked up the hill.

Yes, I can heal most of the symptoms, to say the least. To be honest, I can heal everything if I have enough time, he said.

We were sitting on the edge of the acupuncture bed together, sipping a cup of unusually bitter tea Masaoka had prepared.

You have so much confidence in yourself, I said.

It's nothing to do with confidence. I'm telling you the truth. Self-confidence has no use in front of the truth. Of course, no one wants to visit an acupuncturist who is nervous, you know, the needles and all. But ultimately, there is only one thing to prove our ability, whether you feel better or not.

Can you help children?

Of course.

How about people who don't believe in acupuncture?

I don't see that kind of people in the city lately but yes, I can. If you think about it, they come here because somewhere in their mind they want to believe in me. But it doesn't really matter what they think, just like confidence doesn't matter.

How about pets?

Wealthy folks from Silicon Valley bring their dogs every week. It's pretty common.

Cats?

Yup.

Bunnies?

Sure.

How about hamsters?

I've never treated one but I bet I can.

Fish?

What? Are you joking or serious?

How about emotional pain?

Of course.

How long does it take?

It depends. Wait, we're talking about people, right?

Can you help dead people?

I think you're mistaking me with a voodoo sorcerer.

He laughed and I laughed along with him. I sipped more bitter tea, my legs dangling from the bed.

To tell you the truth, I am relieved that he is gone. I despise him. He left me alone with a small child and debt under my name. I wish I could dig him up to kill him again, I said.

I know.

I am happy because he is gone but I hate him because he is gone.

Right.

I'm pathetic, ugly and . . .

Beautiful.

No, weak.

Weak is bad?

Yes, what else can it be?

That's an idea left over from the Stone Age era when mammoths were still chasing us. Let go of your Stone Age brain. There is no mammoth now. We don't need that survival skill anymore. We're now allowed to be weak, Kyoko. We need weakness.

When mammoths were our prey, the world must have been so simple. Now I don't know what my mammoth is.

Perhaps your husband?

No.

Maybe, you.

I lay down on the bed, stretched my arms wide, and said, No, it's this world!

Wow, you go that far? Didn't see that coming.

A tunnel of sunlight that shone through the gap between the curtains pierced my chest. I had a few more hours with Masaoka before Alex's playdate was over. Just a little longer, I wanted to live in a world where things could be incoherent and irresponsible, where I was allowed to be called weak.

Can you heal emotional pain that you don't even know you have?

Kyoko, that's most people. They come to me when the pain inside manifests in their body. Until then, people don't know that they are hurt emotionally. I don't treat the pain inside them. That's a therapist's job. But I can feel their pain.

You feel it by touching them?

Without touching.

By looking at them?

By sensing the air around them.

Could it be that the needles are just props for you, to look professional or something? Maybe you don't even need them?

What, no! You really haven't tried acupuncture before? If you want, you can try today.

I pushed my body up and looked at Masaoka's face. I tilted my head a little to dodge the tunnel of sunlight. My hair fell on my cheek, and I was under the spell of believing that maybe I could be beautiful like Masaoka said. And even though I knew beauty was a useless quality in my life, I wanted it while I was with him. Was that too selfish?

Wait, but I know a treatment that works better than acupuncture, Masaoka said. The healing that only *I* could give you. Hey, would you like more tea?

He hopped off the bed, grabbed my cup, and walked to the electric kettle. While he hummed an unidentifiable melody, he poured another cup of the bitter tea.

His insolence and self-conceit annoyed me, but the joy of being known by someone filled my heart.

The tea, is this the decocted Chinese herbal? I asked.

Yes.

What kind of effect does it have?

To open up one's heart.

Huh?

Just kidding. This is a good old *Houttuynia cordata* tea. You're so naïve, Kyoko.

When we had spoken long enough to finish two cups of tea, Masaoka tucked my hair behind my ear. With that, I shut my mouth. Just like during the phone call, he slowly opened my blouse button by button, like he was making sure none were loosened. The blouse fell on the floor and our eyes met. Masaoka pressed his lips on my forehead, one long and gentle kiss. I wrapped my legs around his waist, drawing him to me. My hands grabbed each side of the bed behind my hips, my chest wide open. He placed his cold hands on my bare back. My gasp, somewhere between shiver and heaven, escaped. *How could he keep his hands so cold for me even after two cups of warm tea?* It must be his kindness. He breathed deeply, burying his face in my chest, a much deeper sigh than he'd made through the phone. His breath moistened the skin between my breasts. I stroked his hair. His hand began to blend with my body heat. Acupuncturists' fingers were very delicate. I was healed just by being touched by him.

Come lay down.

I hopped off the bed. He took my hand and laid me on the wide sofa.

He lay down on top of me, but he didn't put his weight on me. He supported his body with his arms and legs. *Please don't leave your existence on my body.* This was another rule I had demanded of him. I loathed men's weight, the scent of aftershave, and especially the smell of dry saliva. I wouldn't be able to enjoy myself just thinking about how they would contaminate me.

Masaoka went down on me slowly, savoring every inch of my skin on the tip of his lips and fingers. He paused on my nipples. His upper lip and lower lip brushed up and down on my nipples. He wouldn't suck on them, only hold them in his mouth, barely touching. I could feel his lips trembling a little. *Please don't leave your existence on my body.* As he was instructed, he was extremely careful not to leave his mark on me.

Have I told you I can tell the color of their nipples by looking at women's lips? Yours were my type. I had imagined them all the time until you took me to the shower room. There were two little bumps, darker ones, hiding under your tight wetsuit.

I would never visit an acupuncturist who observes people's lips like that, I said and smiled.

Thank you for not wearing lipstick. But you must put it on in front of other men, okay? You must hide your beautiful lips from them.

He smiled too, tilting his head.

I arched my back, my arms stretching above my head. I breathed deeply. Before my exhale ended, he slid one arm under my back. His upper body was toned from daily surfing; to destroy or support me, my body would be nothing under his arms. His lips quickly found my armpit, the part he had not touched yet. A sweet shriek escaped my mouth unexpectedly.

Good girl, your body always responds to me so honestly, the opposite of your heart.

That is because I've educated you very well, I said.

You'll never give me credit, will you?

I felt sorry for his body, so I inserted my hand in his pants. He was wanting my hand to lead him to somewhere better, I could feel. Masaoka stared at me. His boyish gaze turned into the beast glare. *Today would be the day.* I read his mind. I remembered my old self, who craved this shift, their eyes, the moment when men lost their control.

I pulled my hand out. *No, this is my time. I'm not letting you have it*. He emitted a tender groan and lay next to me. His fingers traveled down on me, unzipped and pushed down my jeans, and slipped into my misty forest. *I must feel like the flesh of a lychee.* He locked my wrists above my head so as not to let me touch myself, to make myself come. *If only I could let him lick me . . .* I closed my eyes, imagining. He stroked me, my wetness, slowly, then fast, teased by stopping his finger occasionally, and returned to slow motion as he read my facial expression. I breathed with the rhythm of his fingers. He let my hands go, and I held on to his neck tightly and concentrated on the one melting spot of my body, the part that existed only to take me to pleasure. Masaoka, surfing, my son, my story, and even myself didn't matter at the peak of this moment. Only the tip between my legs was present. *Release me from my life.* I gripped the edge of the sofa, his bicep, the back of his head, anything to keep myself together. From my thighs to my toes stiffened. My throat tightened. If I had to wait any longer, my heart would stop, my blood vessels would explode, and I would break into shards. I bit my lips to endure the pleasure. Yes, orgasm and death were the same.

Just when I thought I no longer could hold myself, the sensation like my spirit slipping away from my body suddenly ran through me. I sank into the sofa, losing all my strength. As my lips feather-landed onto his earlobe, I dedicated my last moan to him, in his ear. My last breath—the best atonement I could give him.

Even after I had reached my orgasm, Masaoka didn't stop. Multiple pleasures. This was the difference between men and women. We would never be so cruel as to leave a man alone on Earth. We could repeat life and death over and over while we lived.

I felt his heartbeat on my vagina while Masaoka massaged my thigh and caressed my clitoris with the tip of his nose. He thrust out his tongue to pretend to lick me and I glared at him and shook my head. *No.* Then he combed my pubic hair, dearly, with his lips and rested his head on my stomach, cupping my breasts until I begged him, *take me there again.*

Although Masaoka loved my body so diligently and patiently, his touch had never satisfied me as much as it did over the phone. It was always like that. The orgasm that peaked under my imagination ripened much better than any matured by men. *I know my body more than anyone else. I am the only one who can please myself.*

But there must be more important things than physical satisfaction. I wanted to believe that when I lay next to him. I might not understand it today but maybe next time. So I came back over and over to indulge in the acupuncturist's touch.

One morning after surfing, Masaoka told me in the parking lot.

I want a real relationship with someone who can reciprocate my feelings.

*What the fuck he is talking about?* He is married and declared he would not get a divorce. Relationship? Why does *anyone* need that anyway?

Before I go, I want to tell you one thing, Kyoko. Your husband, I think he was going to live. He thought the time with you would continue forever so he didn't act fast. The mortgage, life insurance, credit card debt, of course, he was irresponsible as a man. But you are still raising his, no, *your* son. Things my ex-wife couldn't do even with me, you do alone. You are starting grad school for the hobby that begins and completes only in your head, the least harmful thing you can choose for your son. If I were you, I'd be bragging to everyone, *Hey, aren't I great?*

*Why does he always declare the most obvious as if it was the most profound thing?*

So stop hurting yourself, Kyoko. When you stop hurting yourself is when you can love me and love your husband again. It's not a sin to love, you know. It's nothing to be ashamed of.

What benefit would there be in loving the dead again? No matter what he said, the only truth was that he didn't want to see me anymore. Men were sly. They always presented a sound argument to give them a reason to run away.

You can forget me, forget surfing, but remember what I said, he wanted to live with you and your son. He didn't mean for it to end. It was an accident.

But was it me who thought he was saying something profound? Maybe Masaoka was really telling me the obvious.

June, the month when a clear sky dominated, before the summer fog and after the rainy season, and the cherry blossoms turned green, was also the month when the ocean temperature was the coldest, and people were beguiled by the weather. Snowboarders came down from the mountains, and the virgin surfers who were deceived by the friendly sky jumped in the ocean. *From now to the fall, there will be a lot of surfers. You've got to learn to find your own waves.*

The words Masaoka said when we were waiting for the next set of waves popped into my head. He had already decided that this was the last time for us.

As always, he was pretentious. He indulged in how he sounded.

I leaned on my steering wheel and watched Masaoka's truck turn right. Unbeknownst to me, my tears overflowed.

Was Masaoka real? I erased the call history every time he called me. I didn't keep him in my phone contacts. Even if things with Masaoka were real, they had happened a long time ago. There was no way to confirm them now.

*A black cat stopped in the middle of the empty street and looked at her. It was almost midnight; she was waiting for a bus.*

*Soon the headlights of the bus appeared from the corner. The cat ran to the weedy lot. She got on the bus. From the window, she stared at the dark parking lot and searched for the cat, but it was impossible to find black in the darkness. She'd heard somewhere before, the trick to tracing your memory is to recall the emotions at that time. But what if you can't access the emotion, how would you recall the memory?*

Perhaps the black cat was a story I made up. Every time I thought so, I opened my journal. The page I had opened repeatedly, I kept a Post-it on that page. Yes, there was a black cat. In the journal I wrote on the train to my friend's house, *The black cat stopped and looked at me. He's gone.* I meant Levi, not the cat. The sentences scattered on the page. The moment I was convinced of his death, I was already writing about it. My confusion and anxiety were inevitable, yet in them, I could sense my excitement, an uplifting feeling that something new was about to begin. It was the birth cry of me being released from the shackles of happiness and regaining my freedom.

The anxious handwriting left indents in the paper. When I touched it, I could feel bumps on the surface. I felt like embracing who I was when I was writing, so I followed the indents and arrived at the previous page.

What was I thinking a day before this storm?

The journal entry was from over two years before the black cat incident. I was letting myself know about the pregnancy. It was before I made the decision to have Alex. The size of the letters was uneven, and the lines of text headed diagonally upward, ignoring the lines on the paper. I was lost in my journal, thinking, struggling, suffering, and excited, not about having a child but about stepping into something new.

Something was wrong. I pinched the Post-it and flipped the page back and forth.

There was no record of the time when I raised Alex with Levi. The years between my pregnancy and Levi's disappearance were missing.

*When I'm too content . . .*

I slumped down on the floor and placed my hands to my sides to keep myself from collapsing. My heart contracted then expanded.

Euphoria and freedom, I still hadn't learned how to live with both.

# ひがんばな "Red Spider Lily"

*UNTITLED*, MY FATHER WROTE WITH THREE SETS OF PHOTOS HE SENT me. I'm starting to forget Japanese, so I texted him back *what was the name of the flower in the pictures?* He replied ひがんばな and wrote me, *Narcissus in Spring, Iris in Summer, Spider Lily in Fall, this little shrine kept me entertained on the way to my work.*

———

Since my father retired last year, he had acquired a new hobby— taking pictures on his phone and sending them to me. For fifty years, he commuted to the same office, taking the same bus every day. I imagined him looking out the bus window, noticing the changes of colors in the garden, his heart leaping with the sight of the flowers— small beauties neglected by everyone else but him. He was a man who could notice true joy in his life. Suddenly the image of a small child glued to the bus window came to my mind, and I thought of how adorable my father was.

———

The sound of the name of the flower saddened me. The sound ひ (hē) can mean "tragedy" in Japanese, and がん (gun) has the same pronunciation as "cancer." But when we put both sounds together, ひがん (hēgun), the meaning changes to "the dearest wish."

No matter which way I looked at it, the word pointed me to sadness.

———

The last set of photos were of my mother in front of the red spider lilies. I was sure that he forced her to smile. She was having surgery in a week.

"I cannot believe I got sick before him!" she said.

I don't think he saw that coming, either.

———

I had been avoiding my mother for months, ever since she sent me a photo of a bearded JFK Jr. with the caption JFK JR. STILL ALIVE! HELPING THE PRESIDENT WIN! The two exclamation marks and digestible sentences. A woman who used to write eloquently enough to convince famous singers to respond to her fan letters had adopted the style of her new passion's writing. Once she even waved a fifty-page printed document in front of the screen at me while we were on a video call and said that bad politicians were kidnapping children all over the world to molest them. I've got the evidence here, she said. She warned me I should keep an eye on Alex, who was now probably stronger and smarter than most politicians.

———

*My mother isn't the same person I knew. We need to stop her,* I told my father on the phone.

He laughed and said, "It's because her boy band canceled their concert this year, she needed to direct her passion elsewhere. You know when she is obsessed with something, she devotes her life to that. But it will pass, just like all the other things she has loved."

They weren't technically a boy band. The average age of the men in the group was forty-five, older than I was. I thought about correcting my father, but that didn't seem urgent compared to her brainwashed mind. So I said instead, "You don't know how scary this is! In America, people are getting divorces and families are breaking up because of that. This will destroy us. By the time this election is over, we won't have Mom. We'll have a woman who wears *the* red baseball cap until her hair falls off. Couldn't she find a better thing to be obsessed about?"

"Don't worry. She isn't going to join a cult or protest. I'm here with her," he said and laughed again. Hopeless! Now I had a mother who was marrying into the conspiracy theory and a father who believed his devotion could win her heart over the most "powerful" man on the earth.

I switched my tactic to combat my MAGA mom by messaging her about what she used to care about the most. I wrote to her about Alex's college choices, Bubbe's surgery, and the best eyebrow product I'd found online. Her responses were variations of *yes, nice, good, fine.* Mom, me, and eyebrows, and no enthusiasm! Our exchanges became sporadic as the months went on. Was she finally giving up on her daughter for someone she didn't even know existed until a few months ago?

She eventually stopped replying to my messages altogether. The presidential election had sucked her soul out of her. I mentally began to prepare, letting go of the old image of my lovely mother and trying to accept who she had become. Just when I thought I'd mastered the art of nonattachment, she wrote me an email. The subject line read, *I have stomach cancer.* In the email she explained how the doctor had found out and that she was doing well. *The doctor caught it early enough. I'm very lucky,* she wrote. Then, the last line of her email read, *Please take care of your health.*

———

What kind of person worries about someone else's health when her health is in danger? My mom.

What kind of person stays silent until she has all the pieces together so that you won't spend every minute worrying *what if, what if*? Mom.

———

I immediately hopped on a video call.

She answered, "Don't worry. I'm still eating well. The hospital is ten minutes away by bicycle, and it's clean, and I've got a great doctor there. They even let me come a few days before the surgery so it will be like staying at a hotel. I've downloaded lots of concert videos of *NetsuNetsu.* I can be with them all day without interruptions from your father. I'm all set."

We spoke about Mr. J, the lead singer, who she was in love with. She told me that a few days ago at the rescheduled concert, she had paid for the extra service, a photo shoot with Mr. J. Through the clear acrylic barrier, she articulated her words clearly as she told him that this could be the last concert she might be able to come to because she had cancer.

"You know what he said to me? He said, *Please write me a letter and send it to my agent. I promise, I'll write you back.* Isn't he the best?"

I responded, "He sounds like a nice man."

Behind her, I saw my father walking into the kitchen. The video call ended with my father telling her her lunch was ready.

Soon after, I texted my father, *please take care of my mom.*

He wrote me back, *she is the dearest, most important woman in my life. Of course, I will.*

At that exact moment, my mother was sending me photos of Mr. J. She wrote, *isn't he the best?*

I wrote her back, *yes, he is.*

———

The hospital didn't allow my father to visit my mother, and she didn't answer my phone calls because she was sharing a room with another woman and didn't want to disturb her.

"But don't worry. I see her every day, and she looks well," my father said.

"How?" I asked.

"I bike to the outside of the hospital and call her phone. She looks out the window and waves at me and I wave back."

"You do that every day?"

"Twice a day."

"Twice!"

"I'm retired. I have nothing else to do."

Without realizing, they were having a Romeo and Juliet moment—the pandemic being their obstacle.

———

ひがんばな stands for "passion," and "the only one" in Japanese floriography. I don't think my father knows that.

"Untitled" is more accurate. How else to describe what he has

236 | Yukiko Tominaga

for my mother? "Passion" or "the only one" isn't going to be enough. I return to the last photo my father sent me, and because I am under my father's spell, I see my mother as a cute, sweet girl, and I wonder if this is how my father saw her when he first met her, and now in front of the blossoming red spider lilies.

Then for the first time in a long time, I breathe in the word "love" and hold it in my lungs. The word scratches my chest, trying to get out of me. I want to take my heart out and throw it at a wall. *Breathe.* If I could only stand this feeling, I could own it again. *Stay there, don't run away.*

# There Was a Moment

THEY WAITED FOR THEIR DEPARTURE AT THE SAN FRANCISCO AIRPORT food court. The mother sat at the café while her son walked aimlessly, and her husband followed him. It was a quiet morning. There seemed to be no one flying out from the international terminal at this time of the day.

The son stopped and reached for his father's index finger. He pulled his father with all his weight, pointing at the escalator with the other hand. He had bowlegs and was still learning to run. The son was eighteen months old. The son and his father walked to the escalator. The son had almost fallen on the ground twice, and his father saved him both times. "I got you," the father said. He was proud. How easy it is to be my son's hero! he thought.

In front of the escalator, the father scooped his son into his arms and hopped on. The mother saw her son's face pop up from behind his father's shoulder. The mother waved at him. The son didn't wave, he just held his father's shoulder.

The father's head disappeared behind the edge of the ceiling, then the son's forehead, his nose, and his chin, and in the end, the father's shoes were sucked into the ceiling.

Without them, the house would be too big for him and his dog, the father thought. This was the first time he would be away from his baby and his wife. Once he was back home, he'd change his clothes to work on his car. The 1964 Chevy Impala needed some love before he could resell it. He, his dog, and the old Impala, maybe staying home without his family wouldn't be so bad. He would eat whenever he got hungry and sleep whenever he was tired. He would collect the Chinese delivery boxes a day before garbage day, like when he was a bachelor. No sit-down dinner and no putting his baby to sleep sounded not too bad. But as soon as he'd find his son's blue bear onesie pajamas in the laundry basket, he'd stop his life to hold the onesie to his nose. His son's smell was indescribably sweet. He'd take the onesie to sleep with him every night. If there were baby-smell-flavored jelly beans, he would eat them every day. That could be his new business. Baby-smell candles, baby-smell lotion, sold at BabyScent.com. I bet people would buy them, he thought. But perhaps only his son had this smell. The father had never noticed the baby smell before. His son might be the only one who possessed this special scent.

From her café seat, she could see the escalator. The father's shoes reappeared, his knees, the son's back, then the father's face and the back of her son's head. When they stepped off, the father pointed at the mother. The son waved at her. She waved back, her hand close to her chest. Then, back on the escalator, the father and the son went up. As she watched their heads disappearing, the mother held her breath. Between the escalator noise and the airport announcement, the mother wondered if it was a good idea to leave her husband home alone. Her heart and the escalator kept the same pounding beat, though everything else seemed to stop its motion. An unsettled feeling in her stomach brought the image of tangled worms to her mind.

When she was about to dive into her wormy thoughts, the father, who had ended his journey with the son, came back to her.

"Is it time?" he asked.

She nodded.

The father held the son tight. The son writhed while his father pressed his nose close against his son's ear.

She took a picture of them.

"How am I going to survive without you guys?" the father said.

"It's only six weeks," the mother replied.

"Please call me when you get there. Promise?" the father said.

Nodding, the mother placed her hand on the father's forlorn face. He rested his face on her hand. The mother told herself to remember this moment, his skin, body temperature, and the love that had led her to this series of adventures.

The father carried the son to the security gate. The mother and the father sandwiched their son and hugged each other.

The mother showed their passports and entered the security checkpoint. She placed her luggage on the conveyor belt and her shoes in the bin, then turned back. The father was waving at them. The mother made her son wave back to his father.

The mother and the son went through the metal detector together. While she waited for her carry-on to come, the mother turned back again. The father was crab-walking, moving side to side, waving at them with both hands. The mother waved back. She took her bag and put her shoes on and turned back. The father was gone. The mother stood on her toes to see over the crowd, but he wasn't there, so she bent down to look at the escalator. She saw the father's shoes ascending into the top. *He's gone.* She must catch him, she thought. But the mother couldn't let go of the expensive airplane tickets her husband bought for them. *Silly of me, it's only six weeks,* the mother said to herself.

"Bouken, bouken." The son spoke the Japanese word he'd recently learned.

"That's right, we're going on a big adventure!" she said. As soon as she put him on the ground, he toddled and then ran, so the mother quickly walked after him.

She never turned back.

# ACKNOWLEDGMENTS

My book wouldn't be without you:

Martha Wydysh, for helping for two years to shape my manuscript. You are the most calm and hardworking agent. Exchanging my manuscript every three months with you was pure joy.

Sabrina Pyun, for giving my book all your attention. I think I used up all my luck when my manuscript unexpectedly landed on your desk. I am so lucky.

Peter Orner, my mentor, greatest friend, and family; whenever I was at a dead end with my writing, you showed up. One day, I'll find a way to thank you better.

Scribner team: Dan Cuddy, Susan M. S. Brown, Dana Li, Jaya Miceli, Kassandra Rhoads, Sophie Guimaraes, Brian Belfiglio, Kathy Belden, Nan Graham, and Kate Kenney-Peterson. It was such a joyful experience to work with you all.

San Francisco State University creative writing department, for giving me full aid to go to school. Maxine Chernoff, for your confidence, *It's not a mistake that you are here, because I don't make mistakes,* and calling the chair of the ESL department to find me a private tutor.

*Transfer, Kyoto Journal, Passages North, Oxford Magazine, North*

*Dakota Quarterly, Chicago Quarterly Review,* and *Bellingham Review,* for publishing my stories.

Jack Shoemaker, Jenny Alton, Megan Fishmann, Lena Moses-Schmitt, Alisha Gorder, Dan Smetanka, and everyone at Catapult, for cheering me and supporting me. Jane Vandenburgh, for giving me the idea for the title.

My Jewish family, for teaching me love doesn't care about our cultural differences.

My Japanese family, for giving me such a rich experience growing up. Friends in Japan, Yoshiko Kotera, for always being with me (literally) at my most vulnerable moments; Megumi Kobayashi, for your psychic power and being the auntie to my child; Masako Saito, for your artistic inspirations.

My San Francisco families, who cared for my child like your own and took my child into your homes while I was in school: William family, Christy and Travis family, Inoue family, Madoka Wallace, Yuko and Ian, Nadia Amer, Isa Hershoff-Looper, Susan Howard, Katie and Peter family, Michael and Santi family, Alejandro Maya, Margo Freistadt, Bill Ferguson. Krissy and Charlie Harb, for letting me stay at your café all day to write without buying anything.

My Maui family, Sienna and Kealii family, for sharing the sweetness of being family.

Steve Vermillion, for the first two years, I wrote because you wanted to read my stories. Ira Garde, for our Friday writings. Tim McCutchan, for reading the same story twenty or more times at the pie store. Todd Harman, for introducing SFSU and your artistic support. Wah-Ming Chang and Nila Bhattacharjya, for your morning writing time. Lowkey Reading Party, for encouraging me to write my sketches.

Abi, for putting up with me for all these years. I was your Sancho Panza or you were mine. We drive ourselves crazy, but I'm so happy that you are always next to me.

Steve, without you, I wouldn't have found my loves.